COLONY HIGH

SKY HORIZON SERIES
BOOK 1

DAVID BRIN

COLONY HIGH

DAVID BRIN

CONTENTS

Colony High

By David Brin

Publisher's Note

This is a work of fiction. Names, characters, places, and incidents either are the

COLONY HIGH: SKY HORIZON

By David Brin

For Robert Silverberg

With thanks for a Revolt on Alpha C ...

And in memory of Robert Heinlein and Andre Norton

For tunnels and adventures in the sky ...

And for Jeff ...

SCHOOL IS OUT

Another sharp jolt of displaced air shook the chopper, whose pilot struggled, yanking hard on the stick and throwing his throttle to full. Desperately climbing.

From the other front seat, Dr. Karen Polandres-Behr stared at the vast Garubis ship, perched on three towering legs over a California desert town. Whatever the mighty vessel was doing — manipulating powerful forces – Karen knew it was beyond human experience. The detector console on her lap told her that much, before every dial and screen burned out.

Frenzied queries rattled her ears — frantic demands for information, shouted by officials in New York, Washington and Belize. But Karen could only answer with a low cry as the Garubis tripod trembled visibly. It changed color before her eyes, from reddish to yellow, to green and finally intense blue.

Then, from the alien vessel's rim, there fell a curtain of dazzling light, dripping slowly, as if liquid.

In terrified dismay, Karen saw the radiant cone broaden — catching two nearby earthling aircraft in its hem, melting their rotors and tossing them like gnats, sending them a-tumble toward Mojave dunes. Then the curtain tightened inward, narrowing to fit snugly within the great disk's trio of spindly legs. The fierce illumination seemed to solidify into a bubble of palpable brilliance.

Roaring light heaved around her. Karen held on for dear life as the helicopter dipped, rattled and shook. Alarms wailed. The control panel erupted with red warning flashes. For a minute, all seemed lost.

Then, abruptly, the sensation of powerful energies simply vanished. In seconds the air calmed, releasing her pilot to sob in relief. And Karen's head was out the door, turning. Peering frantically.

A pall of sparkling dust hung over the town of Twenty-Nine Palms, especially the part near Olympic and Rimpau, obscuring everything beneath. Out of this fog, blew a storm of small cylinders – components of the fast-unraveling tripod, now returning to the mothership. Several thousand of the hollow tubes could be seen rushing skyward, joining their fellows in the belly of the giant, hovering disk. Soon all were recovered and the big hatch closed.

With an audible groan, the mighty vessel began climbing away.

"What happened? What happened? What just happened?"

For a moment, Karen couldn't tell where the question came from — a simultaneous chant emitted from her headphones, from everyone in the chopper and from her own dazzled mind.

Then, as the starship started moving, an amplified voice took over the radio waves, every channel and frequency, speaking English with weird, alien tonalities.

Thus, repayment is accomplished.
With this gift, our debt is erased.

Where the tripod had been, just minutes before, a stiffening breeze now tugged at the dust cloud, unraveling it — along with every shred of hope Karen had been vainly clutching. For under the clearing haze, she now saw what had become of Twenty-Nine Palms High School and several surrounding city blocks.

A quiet, crystal clarity settled over Karen's senses. Through headphones she heard someone in authority shout a protest that was immediately translated into Garubis chatter-gabble – the aliens' tongue — as humanity's complaint chased after the fast-departing vessel.

"You ugly space bastards! You call THIS a gift?"

FOUR MONTHS EARLIER…

1

EXTRA CREDIT

Rumors can take on a life of their own. Sometimes, they spread like a virus.

The latest bit of hearsay?

Some of the Math Club geeks have got their hands on a real live alien! They're keeping it hidden in a basement rec room, no less.

Mark had listened to some wild tales while growing up, wherever Dad happened to be stationed at the time. Just as soon as he could pick up some local dialect, Mark would foray to the nearest village or town and tap the gossip mill, fascinated by the bottomless human appetite for preposterous lies. From conspiracy theories murmured in a Lebanese bazaar to scandals about local pop stars, circulating through Manila alleys — the things people believed!

Still, it wasn't till Dad got transferred back to Southern California that Mark realized — there's no place better to breed wild stories than an American high school.

Especially Twenty-Nine Palms High, where the football team mascot, *Spookie,* wore a huge trench-coat, a floppy hat and big black eye-mask. Beyond all the nasty stories that kids typically spread about each other, and hearsay concerning the dating habits of certain teachers, there were always colorful rumors about what went on at the nearby airbase. Or within the top-secret, opaque walls of Cirocco Labs.

But *this* one — about the Math Club guys having an extraterrestrial of their very own?

Well, it beat all.

NOT THAT MARK believed a word of it.

California homes don't have basements, for one thing.

Besides. A captive alien?

Such a cliché. A stupid movie rip-off. Couldn't the nerds come up with a better hoax? Crap, some of their parents worked at Cirocco. What good are brains if you can't be original?

When some of his classmates said they were going over to see for themselves after school, Mark begged off. He had other things in mind. Especially an hour later, staring down at the varsity soccer team —

— *girls* varsity, in blue shorts and yellow tops. They charged across the athletic field in formations as intricate as Dad's squadron during inspection week ... but a whole lot more alluring. The star forward, her tawny legs pumping, somehow made sweat and cutthroat ferocity seem, well —

"Bam?" A voice called to him from above. *"Bamford, what are you doing?"*

The words made him twitch, almost losing his precarious perch upon a stub of concrete, jutting from the wall. Mark dug in with three fingertips of his left hand while probing desperately for a ledge to set his right foot. His heartbeat jolted and spots danced before his eyes like flashing balls.

"Are you all right? Bam?"

"Ye — yeah," he grunted, short of breath.

"Well stop staring at Helene Shockley and focus!"

"Not ... staring ..." he grunted, both irritated and embarrassed. "Slack ... Gimme a lot."

Some tension left the rope, easing pressure from the climbing harness on his thighs and groin, freeing him to lean and traverse, seeking a higher footing. This part of the wall was tricky, designed for competitions in a brand-new league. He would have to master it in order to make the team.

"More slack!" The rope still wasn't loose enough for this reach.

"But ..."

"Come on, Alex ... I'm fighting the clock here. Slack!"

There was time to make up — precious seconds stupidly wasted during that blank stare at the soccer players. Damn hormones.

"Well, fine." She sounded dubious. "But concentrate!"

The rope loosened still more. He bore down, focusing on the task at hand.

Relax, you're in a California desert suburb. No lives are at stake ... this time.

Unlike that cliff in Morocco, when his father had to stay with a critically injured aid worker, sending Mark cross-country for help. One steep shortcut shaved an hour off the round trip ... and Dad later blistered his ears over taking the risk.

The lip of Mark's left shoe found a crevice. Hardly more than a ripple in the wall. He tested it ...

"That one's iffy," commented the voice overhead.

Be quiet. But he didn't have breath to say it. Shifting his weight to the narrow ledge and feeling a sudden burn in his calf, he launched himself upward, reaching ambitiously past a safe hand-hold, grabbing at the last one before the top. For an instant he glimpsed Alex, scowling with concern, her cropped brown hair framed by blue desert sky.

This'll show her I know what I'm —

His hand brushed the knob — the same instant that his shoe slipped. Mark clutched frantically, two fingers bearing all his weight as both legs dangled, desperately seeking a purchase, anything at all. Specks of rough concrete crumbled under the pressure. Pain lanced down his wrist and arm.

"Mark!"

He saw Alex try to reach for him, and suddenly remembered. *I asked for slack. I hope not too much —*

The knob seemed to tear away with deliberate malice — and the ground swung up. Mark glimpsed shouting figures below, scattering out of the way.

Almost too late, the autotensioner kicked in, yanking the safety line hard enough to empty his lungs, stopping his plummet just short of impact. Splayed with arms and legs flung apart, facing the sky like a crushed flower. Like roadkill.

For some unmeasurable time he hung there, tasting acid, blinking away pain-dazzles and struggling to catch his breath till Alex popped the release, easing him down the rest of the way.

Those scattered figures returned, crowding around as Mark's vision cleared — youths who were bigger, stronger and sweatier than most. Well, everyone agreed that the Climbing Wall stood too close to the Free Weights area.

The tallest body-builder leaned over, expressing false concern. "You okay there, Bamford? Want a pillow?"

Jeez. All I need right now is Scott Tepper, Mark thought.

And yet — there was no choice but to clasp the blond senior's offered hand. Better to stand quickly, ignore the pain and try not to groan, even if that meant swaying for several heartbeats.

"You're lucky Coach wasn't here," Scott continued, still looking down at Mark from half a head taller. "He's already ticked off that they put this stupid climbing wall here."

"Yeah," growled Colin Gornet, nearly as towering as Scott but much heavier, pushing close and poking with a finger. But that wasn't what made Mark recoil. The big lineman packed aroma.

"You could've killed somebody, Bamford! When Coach finds out, your 'ascent team' will be history."

Brushing Gornet's jabbing finger aside, Mark glanced at the nearest weight station. It lay at least three meters from the base of the wall. Plenty of room! He was about to argue the point when Scott Tepper raised a palm.

"No need for Coach to find out." He interposed, keeping Colin's persistent arm from poking again. A good thing, since Mark had had enough.

"But Scott, next time this moron falls ..."

"There won't *be* a next time. Will there, Bamford?"

Mark couldn't think of anything to say. Though fuming inside, he knew it was a losing proposition to argue, or compete in any way with Scott Tepper, whose charm seemed to rise out of some infallible instinct. Coupled with good looks and serene confidence, it let Scott manipulate any teacher, win any school office, smooth-talk any girl.

So *much* confidence that he could offer generosity — at a price. *You owe me, Bamford,* said the look in Scott's eyes.

Others were joining the crowd of onlookers, including members of the girls' soccer team. Helene Shockley, tawny and gorgeous, slid up next to Tepper with a questioning smile.

Mark shook his head, eager to get out of there.

"No, Scott. It won't happen again."

ALEXANDRA BEHR WASN'T AS easy to deal with.

"Do you have any idea how hard we lobbied Principal Jeffers to get that wall? It's our shot at getting some X-Sports accepted inside! You better not blow it for us, Bam."

Mark shot her a glare as they walked toward the bike racks. He'd never liked the nickname — *Bam-Bam* ... later shortened to *Bam* — though its macho quality beat most alternatives. High school could be a social nightmare for any transfer student, especially if you got off on the wrong foot. Anyway, the Extreme Sports bunch had been first to accept him. Mark couldn't skateboard worth a damn, but none of *them* had ever gone trekking in the Atlas Mountains, so it all evened out. Why not help pioneer a new sport at TNPHS?

"It won't happen again," he told Alex.

This time the promise felt sincere. He *had* let her down, foolishly losing focus. In the real world, a slip like that could be fatal. Besides, he needed the ascent team, to boost upcoming college applications. Lacking Alex's grade point average, and a bit short for his age, this might be his one chance to varsity at anything.

"Well, okay then." Alex nodded, accepting Mark's word. She punched his shoulder, knowing uncannily how to strike a nerve. He quashed a reflex to rub the spot.

Dang girls who take karate. Mark had grown up with the type, on a dozen military outposts around the world. Oh, they could be great pals. But a more feminine style also had appeal. Anyway, Alex was only a sophomore — not even sixteen and still gawky. Mark inclined toward 'older women' like Helene.

Unfortunately, *they* went for older guys.

Barry Tang awaited them at the bike racks, his Techno already unfolded with gleaming, composite wheels — hand-made for last year's Science Fair. With unkempt, glossy black hair and a misbuttoned shirt, anyone could tell how he interfaced with Alex — on her non-athletic side. They were both Junior Engineers.

"What kept you two?" Barry asked, a little breathlessly. "I want to show you something!"

Mark groaned.

"Gimme a break, will you? My carcass is still practically twisted in half and covered with bruises. And I gotta be at work by four." Not that he relished bagging groceries. But Dad said any kind of job built character. In lieu of allowance, he pitched in a buck for every one Mark earned himself — mostly for the college fund.

"So? You've got twenty-three minutes, and Food King is right over there." Barry pointed to the supermarket, beyond Jonathan's Shell Station and across the street from Twenty-Nine Palms High.

"Well —"

"Come on, Bam." Alex took the back of Mark's neck with one slim, strong hand and started kneading. "I'll work these knots, if you like."

He suppressed an impulse to brush her away. Alex was a pal, after all. Though every now and then ...

Barry Tang glanced over at the two of them with a grimace of feigned jealousy that was maybe partly real. "Are you *rewarding* this guy for messing up, at practice? Maybe *I* should get some bruises too. Somebody'd rub *my* — hey! Stop that!"

Mark had grabbed Barry in a headlock and was knuckle-digging his temple, not very hard. Just enough to be true noogies. When he protested again, Mark let go.

"Why'd you do that!"

"You were asking for bruises. What're friends for?"

"Well," Barry ran his fingers through his mussed hair. "You know what I meant! Anyway ..." His eyes suddenly widened. "There!"

"Huh?"

"Over there, beyond Olympic!" Barry shouted. "I see one!"

"See what?" Alex asked, releasing Mark's neck just when he was closing his eyes, ready to admit it felt good. By the time he looked up, both of his friends were pedaling ahead, past the alley where denim-clad bikers always hung out after tearing around on the dunes. Mark had to chase after, swerving to avoid a muttering bag lady's junk-laden shopping cart, barely catching his friends near the minimart on Main. Barry jabbed a finger north along Bing Crosby Boulevard, toward the Marine Corps base and a vast expanse of desert beyond.

"I don't see —"

"The van!"

Mark blinked. Indeed, there was a van — dark blue, with windows tinted opaque gray. An oval area along one side had been painted over raggedly, without much effort to match shades. A tarp covered some kind of bulge on top.

"So? I don't see —"

"That color and model, I recognize it from the fleet at Cirocco Labs! There's at least a dozen — maybe more — cruising all over the place. Must've been in a real hurry. See how they just slapped some paint on the company logo? And I'll bet you that blanket's hiding sensors. Maybe some kind of a search radar!"

Barry looked so excited — and happy — that Mark hesitated to doubt him aloud. Especially when Alex cast a warning glance, shaking her head.

Is this going to be like a few months ago, when Barry kept yattering about giant Russian transport planes, landing in the middle of the night?

"Haven't either of you heard all the helicopters cruising overhead the last few days? I can spot two of em *right now*, from where we're standing! See that glint near the horizon?" He swiveled. "And there beyond the RV park, over Joshua Tree. They must be looking for something!"

Mark and Alex shared another glance. Neither of them had to say it. In Twenty-Nine Palms, the sight of copters flitting about was as surprising as spotting your own shadow. "An exercise," Mark ventured. "Hotshots from Pendleton —"

"My parents *have* been nervous about something, the last few days," Alex murmured. "When I asked about it, they went all weird on me and clammed up."

Mark shot her an accusing look. *You too?*

Then something occurred to him.

I haven't seen Dad in two days.

Oh, that alone wasn't troubling. It happened several times a year. A note on the fridge, plus an envelope with some cash. No instructions. Just implicit confidence that Mark could be trusted to take care of himself for a while.

Only now he found himself worrying. *Could it be an alert?*

With so many hot spots in the world, units were always being called up and sent to far places that he never heard of, fighting in little scraps that never got called 'wars.'

He didn't recall anything in the news that seemed threatening. No looming crisis. But folks at the nearby base — and at Cirocco Labs — might be involved with something on the horizon, acting long before the media or public got wind of it.

"I joined the Math Club for a while, when I was a freshman," Barry said, his voice cracking slightly. "I still know a couple guys. We play chess now and then."

"So?" Mark just knew he was going to regret asking. Then the connection dawned on him ...

... those silly rumors. *Oh, no.*

"So," Barry finished. "You guys want to find out what's going on?"

It turned into one hell of a Thursday night.

When Mark got off work around seven, he went home hoping to find his dad there, smelly and unshaven from a three-day field trial, but happy to tell his son the unclassified parts over coffee and an omelet. Something that would explain eerie vans and nervous helicopters, even the bizarre rumors sputtering around town, putting it all down to scuttlebutt and normal Defense Department weirdness.

But no. Dad wasn't home.

Instead, Mark found Alex and Barry waiting for him by the battered old Cherokee. Barry held a steaming bucket of drumsticks from *Chick-tish-n-Protie.* Alex must have already let herself in the house, to fetch keys to the jeep. She tossed them at Mark, as soon as he parked his bike.

"You don't waste time," he commented.

"Life's short." It pretty much summed up her philosophy.

What could he do but shrug and climb into the driver's seat? These two had been his best friends since moving to this desert oasis.

They had nursed him through those grueling Chemistry and Trigonometry midterms, making it hard to refuse, even though his body ached and there was school tomorrow.

"Here, swallow this," Alex ordered, handing him a pill – a Motrin, he saw – and a water bottle. Heck, did the girl think she was his mother? But Mark tossed back the muscle relaxer, which seemed a good idea. He shrugged off the bottle.

There's a quiz tomorrow in pre-calc, but Alex drilled me on that chapter during lunch and I ought to get my usual B. Mr. Castro will be holding a discussion on the Thirty Years War, though I guess I know the subject well enough to say something in class, after watching that Tim Burton film about it. Though if I studied a bit more ...

He pictured Helene Shockley, occupying the seat behind him in World History, always wearing some pheromonic scent that would fill his nostrils and send his head spinning. At times, Mark fantasized winning her over with some clever quip or insight in Castro's class. If there were even a *chance* of impressing her —

Forget about it. She's with Scott.

In fact, Mark had to admit, school was under control. He could afford a little week-night adventure.

"Where to?" He asked, starting up the engine.

Barry pointed east. "The dunes. Near Skull Rock. That's where Chloe said they found something, before she clammed up tighter than a trillionaire's wallet."

CRUISING in that direction down Highway 62, they swiftly left behind both the town and the sprawling Marine Corps base to the north that hosted Cirocco Labs. To their right, Joshua Tree National Park rolled by, with its namesake plants resembling spiky warriors by the light of a waxing gibbous moon. A scattered army of those shadowy figures stretched across the plain toward dun-colored hills.

The dry air was cooling down quickly from today's oppressive heat. Mark always liked this part of the evening, here in the high desert. That is, he would have enjoyed the drive if Barry weren't constantly reaching forward from the back seat, tapping Mark on the shoulder and shouting.

"*There!* Another helicopter ..." he pointed urgently, "and one more off by the mesa!"

Mark overcame his irritation to glance that way. And yes, there were aircraft out there, crisscrossing above the sand and scrub. So? Helicopters and drones and such ... next to Twenty-Nine Palms Air Station? Ooooh.

Though ... yes ... they *were* aiming searchlights downward, moving at low altitude, in what did kind of look like a search pattern.

Alex reminded him – twice – about the turnoff to Skull Rock. *I would-of remembered,* he growled inside while turning off the main highway onto a barely-graded dirt road, easy enough for the Cherokee to handle.

We seem to be headed right for one of the helicopter search grids.

"Suppose they really are searching for something. Do you think it's wise for us to be –"

Alex shouted and Mark yanked the wheel hard, briefly blinded by headlights ahead, looming suddenly around a sharp bend. A pickup truck veered by, much too close, while five or so rowdies hollered and screamed from the back. Something hurtled toward Mark and he slammed the brake just in time for a beer bottle to shatter on the hood of the jeep, instead of his face.

"Jerks," Alex muttered, with endearing understatement. "I guess this means we're not the only ones chasing rumors. The only civilians, I mean," she added, glancing toward one of the throbbing helicopters.

Mark pushed the clutch and re-engaged the transmission in low, taking the curve slowly... and pulled aside again for yet another pair of headlights. This time it turned out to be a little Geo Metro – one of the solar-charged conversions that really shouldn't be out after dark; they'd be lucky to make it back to town. Whining and complaining in the grit and dust, it pulled up alongside the Cherokee and the window came down, with an unhealthy, grinding sound. The driver leaned out – a girl Mark had seen around TNPHS, with stringy, braided hair, glasses, a great figure – Isabel something...

"There's a roadblock ahead," she said in all-business tones, though with a nervous edge. Mark couldn't make out her companions, cramped together in the dim cab. "They're turning kids back and taking down names."

"Thanks. Though can you tell us what *you* think is going —" Mark started asking, but the Geo was already speeding off, spewing grit in its wake. He turned to look at Alex and Barry. "Maybe we better think about —"

Alex agreed by both nodding and pointing ahead of them, where a trio of vehicle lights could be seen heading their way, weaving along the road's sinuous path. From the pattern of head-lamps and spot beams, he could tell they were Newts – New Utility Vehicles, capable of switching from wheeled travel to charging cross-country on a cushion of air. You didn't want to argue with guys driving stuff like that.

His passengers made no complaint about the failure of the mission as Mark turned around and headed back to the highway.

Only when they were approaching Twenty-Nine Palms again did Barry finally speak up, apparently back in chipper, hyper-curiosity mode once again.

"All right, then. That pretty much confirms that something big is afoot! Now let's go to our natural habitat and hunt for the truth. I know just where to start. Rimpau Avenue."

PILOTING the Cherokee's stiff old suspension toward the west end of town — where the supposed visitor from space was rumored to be hidden — Mark thought. *If there's any truth to this, it's the worst-kept secret since the Vice Principal got a hairpiece.*

He kept passing cars full of teens — some from TNPHS and others from Mojave College. It felt more like Saturday than a school night.

Alex waved at some guys wearing helmets and pads, who zipped along on gleaming pairs of powered sneaker skates — the latest fad — slower than cars, but a lot more fun and great for shortcuts whenever traffic got dense.

"Hey 'Cardo. Sup!" Alex shouted as one of them came swooping by to slap a friendly palm on the Jeep's hood.

"Hey girl," the wiry boy answered as he spun around once then gave her fist a friendly punch. "Seen *it* yet?"

"It?"

"You know... *it!* Some of us are high on the waiting list. We're all taking bets whether it's real."

"No way, man!" said another skater, barely missing a minivan that swerved into the left turn lane. Mark liked these guys, but they were crazier than kava-chewers.

"I bet it's a rubber puppet," the second one sneered. "Like that robotic thing, last Halloween."

"Yeah? Well Benito Gomez got close last night and he says —"

"Benny's mind is torqued from too much gaming, man. Can't tell what's real anymore. Come on, what're the odds?"

"Yeah but whatif? Hella sick. Deathbed sick! They're only letting a few visitors at a time and you gotta have cash. But I'll put in a good word for you, Alex. Maybe get your friends in —"

A warning bloop from a police car interrupted the skater, who shrugged with a blithe grin. Spinning 360, he did a Parcour tracer's vault over the boulevard's center divider and was gone in a flash of turbo-luminescent rims.

"Get us in *where?*" Alex shouted after him, in vain. Cops didn't even bother chasing the X-guys anymore. They could dart through an intersection and vanish like smoke.

Something's up, all right, Mark thought as he followed Barry's hushed directions along one dismally similar suburban side street after another. *The whole town feels it.*

Or at least the part that was tuned into coolstuf — the mesh of interests approved by those between fifteen and twenty. You didn't have to log into Bellybook or some avachat room to get a ruling on what's hot or not. It splattered like rain across percept-space, a spray of half-sentence twops scrolling down specs and wrist-pads. It murmured into earpieces and pen-cells and swarmed over the fold-screens or pullscreens of pocketphones.

Okay, this is way, way cut, Mark admitted, grudgingly. Whatever it turned out to be — probably a hoax — somebody deserved cred for the town's best mobilization since he came to TNP. Even better, the world of adults appeared clueless. So far – at least here in town — this whole thing seemed limited to the young.

I take that back, Mark thought suddenly, pulling the jeep over to one side. Just ahead, a police car had parked along the very block where Barry said the vice-president of the Math Club lived. Two officers were just getting out, slamming doors.

With a hiss, the black-haired boy pointed.

"Look. There's *two* of those disguised Cirocco vans, just pulling up!"

"This is creepy," Alex said. A crowd was gathering, mostly teens, milling about and peering at the house in question.

"What do we do? Take a look? Join the crowd? Someone outside may know —"

A fist rapped hard on the right-rear door. Barry yelped as a face suddenly pressed against the glass, fogging it with hasty breath.

"Tang! Thank god 'n dog it's you. Open up!"

"What in —" Mark didn't have time to object as Barry let in the figure, swaddled under a cowled windbreaker.

"Drive!" the boy croaked, his visage pale and twitchy.

"But —"

"Get out of here! Then I'll explain."

Against his better judgment, Mark put the car in gear, turning carefully so as not to attract attention. His uninvited passenger sighed, quivering as he looked back at the commotion.

"Alex and Mark, this is Tom," said Barry. "Tom Spencer. That was *his* house with the police car in front."

Alex reached around, offering her hand to the nervous sophomore. "What's up? Want something to drink? We have Pepsi. Or a drumstick?"

Good move, Mark approved, offering a frightened person something as commonplace as food. Though he kept blinking rapidly, the Spencer kid seemed to calm a bit as he slurped a can of soda.

"They... came less than an hour ago. Just busted right in and *took* him!"

"Who came? The police? Didn't they just arrive?" Alex kept her voice scrupulously calm as the boy shook his head.

"Jocks! It was Colin Gornet and some of his football pals!" In the rear-view, Mark saw Tom take another long slurp, before resuming his rapid babble. "They came by for the first time last night, polite as could be. Paid me *fifty dollars* to let them in. Just wanted to have a look, they said. I should've listened to Jamul. He told me not to! But fifty will help buy that new hacking algorithm I wanted all year. So I let 'em in. Idiot!" He kicked the door next to him, reverberating the Jeep's rickety cab.

"Chill, Tom. You say they paid you to let them look at something. *What* did they pay to see?"

But he was chattering now, telling it his own way.

"By this morning, it seemed like every kid in town knew! People kept sneaking up to my back door after school, offering *more* cash for a look at Xeno. It felt cool for a while, till Gornet and his bunch came back. They crashed right in and grabbed him!"

"*Who* did they grab?"

Tom Spencer shook his head.

"Then it got worse! My parents heard us yelling as Gornet left. They saw Gavin's black eye and found the mess downstairs... *so they called the cops.* I couldn't stop them!"

Mark shook his head. Clearly this dude had a hierarchy of fears. Invasion by thieving athletes was intolerable — but not half as bad as alerting the world of adults.

"All right," Alex asked, her voice glassy-smooth, to keep the frantic boy calm enough to communicate. "You're saying Gornet and his pals came barging in and grabbed someone. But who, Tom? Who did they take?"

Mark found himself fervently hoping that Tom would just shut up.

It's just a hoax that got out of hand, he hoped. *It's got to be.*

Tom swallowed hard before answering.

"They took our xenoanthropoid."

"Your —?"

Barry Tang translated. "It's Greek, meaning something like 'a manlike being from beyond.' Pretty awful Greek, actually. I guess they wanted something less cliched than *alien* or *extraterrestrial.*"

Tom sniffed.

"We spent days coming up with that! Anyway, it's a damn good thing we were the ones who found him. Well, Chloe Mendel did, while she was performing one of her routine comet-searches. The IR scanner on her 22-inch wide-field telescope spotted something coming in fast."

"Nobody at the base saw it?"

"Her correlator noticed something all those Cirocco brainiacs missed!" Tom snorted, both proud and contemptuous. "I guess because it had all the color values of a falling meteorite. Anyway, a fresh carbonaceous chondrite is worth heaps, so Chloe called me and Jamul and Jorge and Lauren to check the fall site, out in the southeastern drifts. Only when we got there, we found..." The boy's hands shook as he gestured, shaping something rounded, almost as if he could still see it, right in front of his face.

"... we found a *space capsule of some kind,* half embedded in one of the dunes! Debris nearby. A panel, like some kind of escape door had popped off..."

"No way!" Barry sighed, in a tone that was almost reverent and hushed. He prompted. "Then —"

"Then we found *him...* wandering around on the sands."

MARK SHOOK his head as he drove, silently wishing.

Please make it stop.

Oh, part of him shared the excitement, a natural yearning for something exceptional to happen. Anything more interesting than the ennui of semi-rural American teenage life, warehoused in a high school routine that often seemed meant just to use up time, keeping youths occupied at an age when biology made them want to *move!* To experience and have adventures. In other eras, frontiers and unknown lands used to beckon. Today?

Small wonder that first contact with some kind of alien race was the stuff of so many vids and modern legends, occupying a place in modern hearts that used to be devoted to mythological beasts and exotic foreign princesses.

But really, how likely was it for some star-visitor to show up right now? Science had never found a single trace of intelligent life. No radio messages from the stars, nor any verifiable evidence of visits to Earth, not even in the planet's deep past.

None of this made sense.

Why here? Why now?

"So you took this... entity to your basement," Alex summarized, her voice low and disbelieving.

"After burying the capsule and covering our tracks." Tom Spencer nodded. "My rec room seemed best, since my parents never come down there. Boy, was *that* an all-nighter! But by morning Chloe had our xeno guest surrounded with a kick-ass audio-visual translation system. We tried every language you can download from the Web."

"How'd that go?" Barry asked eagerly.

"Not so good. So we backtracked and started over with permutation math. You know, universal stuff that any technological species oughta know. There are even some programmed scenarios, pre-worked out by amateur SETI clubs —"

SETI, Mark translated. *Search for Extraterrestrial Intelligence.* Yeah, it fit.

"And?" Barry was barely touching his seat, bouncing from excitement.

"And? Well, things got pretty frustrating! None of the stuff we downloaded seemed to work. None of the math or geometry or symbol stuff. Or web picture shows. For one thing, we had trouble getting Xeno's attention. He wasn't in great shape. Jorge offered all kinds of food. Thank God n' dog he took a sudden liking to marrow."

"Marrow?"

"The stuff inside bones, that makes red blood cells and —"

"We know what marrow is," Mark snapped. He was starting to get angry. And he realized something else.

I've been driving without thinking ...

... toward Colin Gornet's house.

It was in the best neighborhood of Twenty-Nine Palms — sometimes called "New Palm Springs" — where spacious homes sprawled amid heaps of non-native greenery ... lush plants and trees that drank water by the acre-foot. Mark knew the place with a nagging sense of personal hurt. Shortly after he transferred to TNPHS, someone ambiguously invited him to drop by one of Gornet's parties, where kids at the top rung would be hanging out. Swallowing the bait, he showed up only to be turned away at the door amid raucous laughter from those inside.

Sure, he should have seen the sucker-draw miles away. *My own damn fault if it hurt.*

Anyway, never mind all that. What bothered Mark right now was a sense of consistency to this story. If Gornet and his pals really had taken something — or some*body* — from the math nerds, it would be completely in character. Still, Mark felt little sympathy for Tom Spencer.

"*Why?*" he asked. "Why keep a space alien in your basement?"

Tom answered with a tone of stretched patience, as if Mark's question were completely moronic.

"Because I'm the only one who *has* a basement. It's roomier than Gavin's shed and warmer at night. Didn't I just say that my folks never go down there —"

A frustrated gurgle filled Mark's throat. With a glance his way, Alex took over.

"No, Tom. The question is — why didn't you call somebody? NASA. The Air Force. State Department. The press?"

Tom blinked, as if unsure he could be hearing her right. As if the question made no sense at all.

"But ... but ... he's ours!"

For a slender youth, Tom's jaw set with grim determination.

"He's ours, and we're gonna keep him."

ONCE TOM GOT STARTED, there were plenty of rationalizations.

"We hid Xeno in order to save his life! Those government guys would only dissect him the minute they got their hands on him."

Sure, Mark thought sarcastically as he swung into Bryer Estates. *Cut up a star-alien. You'll learn lots that way. More than, say, by asking questions.* But Tom wasn't finished.

"Those guys would just take him to some secret underground lab and hide him forever!"

Again, Mark shook his head silently.

Maybe. But to study an alien technology you'd need hundreds of skilled people — maybe thousands — the very best, with open minds. The kind of top professionals who question assumptions and resent needless secrecy.

What's to stop any of them from leaking proof of a coverup? Fear? When they'd become big whistle-blower media stars?

It was always the same with all UFO or "Roswell" type cult stories. They invariably assumed that the very brightest members of a free society were all drones or fools or tools.

Mark envisioned someone trying to cram Dad into a category like that. *Yeah, right. He always told me that the most effective, best-disciplined soldiers are those who understand the reasons. Blind obedience is for machines.*

"The government would *have* to keep this kind of thing hidden from the public," went Tom's next rationalization, one he must have rehearsed among his friends. "The potential for mass hysteria is unimaginable!"

Now he's quoting from some movie, Mark thought.

Funny how everybody is always sure that their own in-group can handle disturbing news, but that people in general would riot or go mad.

Sure, I'm kind of shocked — but I also feel ... focused. Either this is a great big hoax, designed to make the whole town look stupid, or —

— or else our entire world may be changing.

Either way, it kind of gets your attention.

AT LAST, the long chain of clichéd excuses started fizzling out. By the time they parked, a few dozen yards downhill from the stately Gornet home, Tom Spencer was fizzing with schemes to win back what had been taken from him. For starters, he wanted Alex and Barry to contact the other Junior Engineers.

"We mathists should've included you guys from the start," he confessed. "With all those gladiator robots you techies keep building, it should be a cinch to break into Gornet's place. Then pow!" He punched the air. "But first we gotta reconnoiter."

"Gotta what?"

"Check the grounds, figure a way in. Chloe has some great night vision equipment. Let's head over to her place and ... hey! Where are you going?"

Mark stepped out of the Jeep, closing his door softly behind him.

"We're going to *reconnoiter,* like you said," Alex replied with a wry smile, following Mark's example as Tom sputtered and started to protest. Barry grabbed the Spencer boy's shoulder and he lapsed into silence, trailing nervously a few paces behind.

The pavement felt strangely gritty under Mark's feet. Pebbles scraped louder, more vividly than normal, like the hissing sprinklers on a nearby lawn. Mark recognized the sensation. Adrenaline rush. The senses can heighten astoundingly when your comfortable routine has been shattered, replaced by daunting flickers of a new — and possibly hazardous — unknown.

He wondered. Did people feel this way all the time in olden-tribal days, back when the surrounding night held fearsome mysteries, anything from hungry tigers to angry gods? This level of heightened awareness could be dreadful ... or *exhilarating*, an ultimate high. No wonder so many kids were drawn to taking risks. A more natural and thrilling high than any drug.

And yet, most of these high schoolers don't know a thing about real danger, he thought as he led their foursome along the shadowed rim of a long, sweeping driveway. *Most people learn about trouble from movies.*

Mark had some first-hand experience with the real thing. Like that time in Bolivia, when his father's training unit wasn't supposed to bring dependents into a territory known for kidnappings and militia-style killings. But Mom had just passed away and Dad didn't want to leave a grieving boy behind with aunts and uncles. So he swung a student exchange program for Mark in La Paz. Safe enough, it seemed. That is, till Mark and a local kid took that impulsive drive into the mountains, and everything suddenly got intense ....

The Gornet house was a rambling thing built during the recent land boom, when Cirocco Labs set up shop nearby, transforming Twenty-Nine Palms from a sleepy little garrison village into an ultra-tech center for national defense research. The house was made up of several structures linked by fancy, glassed-in walkways — great for formal entertaining. And for keeping bothersome teenagers out of the way around back, where a large guest cabaña stood next to the blue ripple of a huge swimming pool. Mark quickly spotted other kids from TNPHS hanging about, small clusters of seniors and juniors mostly, talking in hushed, excited tones. Cigarette embers flared, here and there, like rebellious fireflies.

Mark recalled the last time he came to this place. There had been loud music and a lot less tension in the air. Still, he felt wary. Could this be another trap? A hoax, designed to draw in whole groups of suckers at a time, like an assembly line? An impressive stunt could make your senior class a legend, recalled with envy by generation after generation of students at Twenty-Nine Palms High.

He glanced suspiciously at Tom Spencer, who might be playing a pivotal role, lending credibility to the spoof. The fifteen-year old honors student licked his lips nervously. His earlier look of combative determination was giving way to anxiety.

Could he be acting?

Maybe. If it was Drama Club instead of Math Club. But I'd bet my chances of ever getting a sports car that he's genuinely scared right now. And pissed-off over losing something precious.

An honest-to-gosh alien? Maybe not. Probably not. But something.

Mark and Alex led the two younger boys past several of the small groups. Eyes flitted and scanned, some of them wearing the new *overlay goggles* – the kind that could scan your face and seek info about you from the web, supplying your name to the wearer, plus anything else he wanted to know about you. Some of the most recent models could even detect chemicals – like what you had eaten – or read your pulse and blood pressure...

... but no one spoke or stepped in front of the four of them, offering a challenge. Not so far.

They approached within spitting distance of the cabaña before two large figures emerged from a heavily curtained doorway. One of them thrust out a burly arm.

"Close enough. You brats got cash? There's a cover."

"A c-cover?" Barry asked. "How much?"

"A hundred just to go in. Twenty a minute for a closer look."

Ouch! Mark thought. He had just the price of one admission in the envelope Dad left behind. *So it is a scam, after all. Whether the story's true or not.*

"What?" Tom Spencer stepped forward angrily, briefly forgetting his fear. "I let five of you in at once, for just fifty!"

The taller figure — Mark recognized one of the school running backs — shrugged with indifference. "We've got expenses. It costs a lot to keep a specimen like this. Call it a contribution for upkeep."

"*Specimen?*" Tom squeaked. "He's an intelligent life form! You're not only thieves. You'll be *murderers* if you keep this up. You don't have any idea what you're doing!"

Another form stepped out of the dimly-lit guest house. This time, Mark recognized Colin Gornet, dressed in khakis and a black turtle-neck. He felt Tom Spencer go suddenly iron-tense ... only to jolt back in surprise at Gornet's mild, offhand tone.

"Hey Spencer. I'm glad you came. Sorry things got a little rough at your house. But you were being stupid and we had to act fast. Anyway, we need to talk, you and me. Right now."

Gornet barely glanced at Mark, Alex and Barry. "Your friends can go right in, to make sure the xeno-thing is all right."

He assumes we're members of Tom's bunch, Mark realized, unsure whether to feel glad ... or insulted over being mistaken for one of the Math Club domes.

Stunned by Gornet's sudden cordiality, Tom stared up blankly as a beefy hand took his arm, leading him over to the pool. Soon he was nodding as the big senior spoke, motioning repeatedly toward the guest house.

"Come on." Barry tugged at Mark and Alex. "Before they change their minds!"

The door guardians scowled at the idea of giving out freebies. "Don't throw anything or raise your voices," one of them warned, holding back a thick curtain for Mark and the others to enter. "And the next guy who pokes it with a stick is gonna be sorry."

MARK'S EYES took some time adjusting to the dim light inside, made even more difficult by a single pinpoint, glaring from one corner of the room. The source, a small but intense spotlight, shone outward from a large cage — the sort made for big dogs in a kennel.

Moving closer, he sniffed fresh redwood shavings ... then a musty, wet smell of uncooked meat ... and finally something else. An aroma unlike anything he ever encountered in his travels.

The cage had some furnishings. Two television sets flickered with the sound turned down low, one of them showing a children's cartoon program while the other featured some kind of stock car demolition derby. Paper and crayons lay untouched on a low table. Mark noticed what looked like the remains of an old-fashioned tablet computer, ripped into several pieces.

Alex nudged him toward the opposite end of the enclosure. Mark had to force his reluctant body, head and gaze to turn.

A shape stirred there, about the size of a ten year-old child — or maybe a chimpanzee. There was something hunched-over about its posture. Clutching a shrouding blanket like a monk's hood, it moved from the far corner as Mark squinted. The figure slowly reached out to take something from a greasy platter. Droplets of dark, dense moisture fell audibly.

Till that moment, part of Mark had nursed the fading hope that it would all turn out to be a hoax after all, a truly first-rate *gotcha,* so clever that you'd tell your kids about it someday, proud even to be one of the dumb suckers who fell for it.

Meanwhile, another part yearned for everything to be true! Something both dazzling and different to shake up this dreary suburban life. A thrill of recognition and affinity with the strange. He had felt it before, in other lands, finding things in common with people who spoke exotic tongues in far corners of the globe.

One or the other. A grand hoax or a startling new connection. Either would be fine.

But then Mark watched that limb extend, grabbing a hunk of raw meat, and he knew.

It's got two elbows on each arm. Just one joint on each finger.

And that's not like any skin I ever saw.

And there's nobody this side of Hollywood who could fake moves like that.

A big, dripping rib-eye steak lifted from the platter and vanished under the blanket. There were crunching sounds ...

... then a gobbet of chewed-up meat and bone hurtled toward a nearby bucket, already brimming with bloody detritus.

"Yikes," Alex said.

"It — it *can't* be real," Barry stammered, though he had been the most enthusiastic up till that very moment. Instead of standing in front, he slipped back, a little behind Mark and Alex.

Then the makeshift hood slipped back. From under the blanket emerged a tapered snout, tinged red. It moved in a side-to-side chewing motion that Mark could not remember ever seeing on Animal Planet. The skull was very wide and flat on top. Two forward-facing eyes bulged from either side of the extended jaw. They glittered in the spotlight, with a golden quality that Mark didn't find either warm or cheering.

A faint *chuttering* sound emerged. Strange and unhappy. Or at least, that was how it felt. Then a greasy hand stretched toward them. A multi-digited hand extended, pointing.

It could be asking for help, Mark speculated. *Or saying 'I'll remember your faces.'*

Or that could be a polite gesture where he comes from, meaning 'thanks for all the yummy steaks.'

Or else, he thought, watching the finger twitch at each of them in turn, *maybe that sound is its way of saying 'Bang, bang!'*

Mark tried to quash feelings of revulsion that welled from the pit of his stomach. According to the movies, aliens came in five varieties, monstrous, sexy, silly, god-like or adorable ... or some combination of those clearcut traits. They were supposed to rouse simple emotions — attraction, pity, giggles, awe or dread.

Off-hand, he couldn't recall portrayals of anything like this — so ambiguously weird, so pathetic, yet intimidating at the same time ...

... but also kind of gross.

That was what finally convinced him it couldn't be a ruse. Nobody would try so hard to fake a creature that filled you with confusion. The old clichés — even terror — were more comforting and credible.

Everybody has a coping mechanism. Alex seemed to take refuge in dispassionate scrutiny.

"Binocular vision," she mused. "Very widely spaced hunters' eyes. I'd guess nocturnal predator ancestors ... those jaws ..."

It was the sort of thing Mark might have expected Barry Tang to say. But under stress, it was all Barry could manage just to stammer.

"I can't decide ... w-whether to laugh or hurl."

Mark nodded, agreeing.

Just don't do both at the same time.

"ALL RIGHT, THAT'S ENOUGH," growled a voice behind them. "You can see he's doing just fine. Now you nerds get out."

Mark and Alex had to drag at Barry till his gaze broke from the creature in the cage. "Wait," he babbled. "There's got to be ... some kind of explanation ...."

And he was right. An explanation of a sort awaited them outside, where a suddenly eager Tom Spencer could be seen shaking Colin Gornet's hand. As Gornet turned to stride toward the big house, Tom actually beamed.

"It's all settled!" he told Barry, nodding also to Alex and Mark. "It turns out this was all for the best."

"What do you mean?" Alex asked.

"I mean we should have listened to Colin in the first place! This town is getting way too hot, with all those Cirocco guys prowling around suspicious. We've got to move Xeno, quick! Anyway this is going to require a lot more resources than Chloe and Jorge and I could manage by ourselves. Colin's got contacts in Los Angeles, where you can hide anything! He knows one of the actors on *Rock n' Troll* who has his own place in Bel Air, without interfering parents —"

"But —"

"Colin says *we* can stay in charge of the scientific side, figuring out Xeno's needs and working on a translation program. Gornet and Tepper and their friends will take care of logistics and finance."

Like charging big-time admission to some highly selected urban elite, Mark thought, picturing how this could vault them into partying with Hollywood's bad-boy aristocracy. What better ticket than offering jaded stars something secret and new? Something truly out-of-this-world.

Plus maybe the lion's share of any fantastic reward that may come from assisting a stranded alien to find its way back home. Isn't that the classic scenario? Help it escape the vile grownups who run government and civilization and you'll get a magic ring or sword or something.

The payoff could be limitless.

"But first, we've got to get him out of town!" Tom babbled. "Colin's arranging transportation to a better hiding place —"

Alex blurted, "You've got to be —" but stopped short when Mark grabbed her elbow. It was time to listen.

"*We've* got to work on erasing the trail!" Tom continued. "That means coming up with a believable cover story. So we've decided to pretend it was all a prank all along!"

"Um ... how do you plan to do that?" Mark asked.

"Oh, it shouldn't be too hard. We'll set up something here in the cabaña ... some kind of *fake* alien that moves a bit and makes some noise ... anything to explain the rumors and folks who've already seen it. Convince eyewitnesses they were fooled in the dark. That's where your Engineer Club pals come in, Barry. Can you get a team together and come up with something by morning? Colin promised to cover your expenses!"

Barry blinked a few times, warming to the notion.

"We-e-ll ... I think so. Nothing fancy, of course. But now that I think about it, we got a bunch of actuators and stuff left over from Halloween ... and I know where to get some of that Plastic Flesh goo they use on those mobile, talking store mannequins. In fact, if we started with one of those mannequins ... Britney Chang should be able to swipe one of those from ... You *do* realize, of course, that it won't match the real thing? A lot of guys will remember the difference."

"Let em. That's the beauty of it! Wild stories are just fine. Let people yell coverup all they want. The whole thing could even wind up on some UFO show, like *Mysteries of the Weird!* That won't matter a bit, so long as we make the hoax explanation seem equally plausible. It'll be enough to throw off the scent!"

While Tom and Barry babbled more about how to build a fake

alien in just a few hours, Mark glanced toward the big house. Through a downstairs window, he saw Colin Gornet in a room plastered with music and sports posters, talking urgently on his pen-cell. Others paced and smoked j-stiks, making calls of their own. A lot of organizing seemed to be going on. No surprise there. American teens who couldn't manage simple algebra were capable of highly sophisticated planning, when it came to stuff they cared about — from elaborate parties or trips to student elections. Or else pulling something over on clueless parents. No scholastic test could appraise such skills. They formed out of life experience, the way young cavemen would have learned about prey animals or the lay of the land.

Mark glimpsed Scott Tepper and Helene Shockley, using their own phones on a sofa. So, the very top layer of TNPHS society was involved. In fact, Tepper had probably been using Gornet as a front man, pulling strings all along.

And now, by pure chance, Alex and I are being invited to participate, Mark realized. Maybe two dozen would finally wind up inside. Too many to keep a secret, normally. But with the tribal gulf between generations — helped by a sense of drama and Tepper's charismatic leadership — the conspiracy might hold together. For a while. Long enough to get something going in L.A.

Maybe.

Well, you wanted something special in your life. Something exciting.

He had yearned to be accepted. Nothing was more likely to guarantee it than helping Tepper and Gornet spirit away a creature from the stars, stashing the thing – safe from prying authorities — in some urban hideaway, then assisting Barry and his friends as they focused their considerable talents on talking to the alien-guest. While a vast majority at TNPHS scratched their heads in wonder at tonight's 'hoax', Mark would be part of the core group, right there with Tepper and beautiful Helene, doing something sensational, amazing, important ....

That final word made him blink.

Important ...

... important to who?

While Barry and Tom argued about which supplies might be needed, and whose talents were absolutely essential to the conspiracy, Mark couldn't help remembering that ugly thing under the blanket, at once both pathetic and chilling. Intelligent. And definitely alive.

He thought again about his own excitement over being part of something dramatic, secretive and bold. It was alluring — almost too good to be true.

Question the very thing you want most to believe.

He had once seen that motto in a most unlikely place, carved on the lintel over a modest doorway in a small Mauritanian curio shop. The Arabic expression had taken root somewhere in his brain, now rising up to haunt him.

We're thinking about what's important to us.

To us.

But we don't really matter right now.

In fact, what I want is just about the least important thing in the world.

Mark turned and took Alex's arm, retreating a few steps toward the shadowed drive.

"We've got to talk."

She met his gaze straight-on. And though her face didn't mesmerize him the way Helene Shockley's did, he found something much more helpful right now in her eyes — common sense.

"Are you thinking what I'm thinking?" she asked.

He couldn't bring himself to come right out and say it. The plan forming in his mind right now would finish him, socially, at Twenty-Nine Palms High School. Worse, it would follow him wherever he went, branding him from tonight onward.

Still, he kept picturing the creature in the cabaña, pointing that crooked finger and chuttering strange, alien phrases.

And Mark recalled something else ... something that Clint Eastwood had said, in one of those timeless *Dirty Harry* movies.

"A man's *got* to know his limitations," he murmured out loud.

Alex shot him a questioning look. And Mark shook himself.

"Let's go. We have work to do."

2

SPECIAL ASSIGNMENT

Y ou had to hand it to the Cirocco spooks. When they got a chance — responding to an anonymous tip – they pounced with startling speed.

A little after midnight, six blue vans swept into Bryer Estates, roared up the Gornet family's ornate driveway and pinioned a surprised Tom Spencer with their headlights as black-clad men leaped out. Several of them carried sophisticated gear ... sensors of some kind that they waved about, quickly triangulating upon the little guest house behind the swimming pool.

Other invaders – their faces covered by blur-cloth veils – brandished the latest model of stun-prod, creating an imposing barrier to teenagers spilling out of the main house. The black-clad men didn't exactly *aim* their non-lethal weapons at the kids. They didn't have to. Body language sufficed to keep Scott, Colin and the others back. That, plus the very-lethal Glock pistols that the raiders also wore holstered at their hips, in easy reach.

Brief shouting poured from the cabaña. Then, out staggered the two big football players who had been standing guard inside, clutching their ears in evident nausea. One of them stumbled, took a knee and heaved his dinner into the Gornet swimming pool, before Helene Shockley took his arm, leading the boy away.

Non-lethal – it didn't necessarily translate as fun.

Mark watched the action through a pair of Tru-Vu glasses, provided by one of the passengers in his crowded Jeep... six sweaty adults along with their portable equipment. The scene was transmitted by Alexandra Behr, from a shrub next to the Gornet driveway. Her voice hissed with tension.

"They have the alien, Mark. They're leading him out of the guest house ..."

Displayed on the inner surface of the Tru-Vu specs, the scene that she described was stark before Mark's eyes. Poor Tom Spencer and his friends wailed when they saw their 'xenoanthropoid' tugged gently out of the cabaña — shambling toward an air-conditioned van, with the stained bathrobe trailing behind.

The jocks — including Colin Gornet — were quieter in their disappointment. Though fists were hard-clenched. (Goodbye Hollywood starlets!)

Mark's heart pounded with tension. But he left the decision to Alex, choosing exactly the right moment to put their plan into action.

Even expecting it any moment, her command still made him jump. *"Now Mark!"*

It felt like Morocco, all over again. Especially sweaty palms that slipped over the old stick, the first time he tried to shift into first. Concentrating for calm, Mark eased the clutch, then slammed his foot hard on the accelerator, redlining the thirty-year old engine as he tore along Yucca street, then veered sharply up the driveway –

— swinging the Jeep sideways at the very last instant, just missing the tail bumper of the last Cirrocco van! Now, there was no way for anybody to leave. And Mark made sure, by shutting down the engine and tossing the keys under a nearby shrub. It would take at least several minutes to find them again.

The black-clad spooks spun and crouched in surprise, clearly dismayed to find their exit suddenly blocked ...

... as out from the Jeep spilled the witnesses that Mark and Alex

had spent a hectic hour collecting. Two local TV crews, a hyperblog-
ger, and one grinning high school teacher quickly deployed *their* own
"non-lethal weapons," covering *both* groups – the teens and the men-
in-dark clothes — with spotlights and digicams, transmitting live to
the world. With special attention devoted to the Guest of Honor. A
visitor from across the stars.

The xeno raised one hand to shade its huge eyes – blinking sideways – from the spotlight glare.

Gotcha, Mark murmured within, as Alex emerged from her hiding
place to join him. *Sorry about the ruckus, but it truly is for your own
good.*

There had been no other way around the dilemma. It was one
thing to get the alien out of the insanely irresponsible hands of the
Tepper-Gornet bunch. It had been quite another thing, figuring how
to ensure that it wouldn't simply shift from one bunch of secretive
fools to another.

Pinned by light and by shouted questions from news reporters,
the government agents had no choice then, but to identify themselves. To show credentials and do it all on video, while the junior-
most anchor from Channel Six babbled excitedly, no doubt with
visions of national promotion dancing in her eyes. Perhaps, long ago,
the spooks might have seized cameras, destroyed film evidence or
memory chips. Those days were gone, and they knew it. The scene
was visible from dozens of neighboring houses, with security cams
streaming to the web. Heck, it was probably in view of a commercial
satellite, right now.

You had to hand it to Barry Tang. A minute ago, he had been as
pole-axed shocked as Tom Spencer and the others. Now he chortled
as he ripped covers off parts of the nearest van, exposing a license
plate, then a panel with a Cirrocco logo. "Hey, Mark and Alex! You
see? Was I right? Grab some frames of this."

Mark knew there was no way to disguise what he had done this
evening. And he was going to pay for it. But did Barry *have* to draw
attention this way? While Scott Tepper stood with arms crossed and a
calm, appraising expression on his face, Colin Gornet and two of his

pals turned to look straight at Mark, drilling him with vengeful expressions.

He managed to stand erect in the light, having sworn not to regret this evening's endeavor. While the Cirrocco operatives removed their masks and grumpily answered questions, Mark met Gornet's gaze, remembering what Tom Spencer himself said, just a few hours before.

You'd be murderers if you kept this up.

You just didn't have any idea what you're doing.

Now, as the full impact started to dawn, Mark realized.

I don't either.

I wonder if anyone does?

3

HOMEWORK

In the days that followed, Mark's heart sank with every news report that mentioned his name. Reporters haunted the front lawn, shouting questions whenever he came outside. Every time the phone rang, he felt a tightness in his throat.

Fortunately, Dad handled most calls — the obscene or threatening ones, along with those who offered help.

"No, we don't need police protection," Mark heard him tell the County Sheriff at one point. "I've been given a desk job till this blows over — paperwork I can handle mostly from home. So just leave all the cranks and drive-bys to me. They're mostly blowhards."

Maybe. But some of the phone voices were pretty scary, whispering or shouting threats ... or else making dumb fake-alien noises. Mark didn't bother checking email or the sosh-sites anymore. His text-boxes, eposcenes and wallboards overflowed with messages from all over the world — some approving, but all too many of them anonymous denunciations, expressing ALL-CAPS fury over what he'd done. Meanwhile, Dad took care of the old-fashioned entreaties from the older generation.

"No, my son doesn't need an agent ... sure, I'll keep your number. Goodbye."

"No he's not interested in doing a Reality TV show!"

"No sir, I don't believe you're calling from the Vatican."

"Look, how do I know you're really Bieber ... prove it."

"The governor? Is this really the governor? We've had a lot of crank calls ... er, if you don't mind, sir, how about doing an impression of your father. Say, 'I'll be back.' Now do your great-uncle. Say 'Ich bin ein Ber' – hello? Hello?"

After that last one, Major Al Bamford had grinned sheepishly. "I'm ninety-nine percent sure that was a fake call. If it's not, I could be in trouble." Clearly, Dad was both irritated by it all and trying to make the best of things.

"You don't have to go on limited duty," Mark told his father, who was already in uniform, despite the fact that he'd be working from home today. "Your unit has an important job, now more than ever. I can stay. Watch things here —"

"— and skip school? Not likely." Major Bamford chuckled. "Look, son, I know some jerks may be rough on you today. But you've got to face them. What you did was smart and brave. You thought about humanity and your country, not just a circle of delusional teens. It was the right thing to do."

The right thing?

Maybe. But also painful. At Mark's age, there were few put-downs more devastating than to be called a 'snitch'. Even among those who agreed with his decision, many thought that Mark did it out of self-interest — to grab headlines and become the center of attention. That opinion only grew each time his photo appeared in newzines or the web.

None of the stories got it right of course, or told how difficult the choice had been.

"Go on," his father told him that morning, eighty hours after a fateful Thursday night. "Go to school. Try to have a normal day."

Easier said than done. But Mark knew Dad meant well, and his approval mattered more than anyone's. *Especially since it might just be the two of us again, if I have to transfer schools. Or leave town.*

That seemed increasingly likely, from the moment he swung his bike into the racks at TNPHS, feeling intense looks from everyone he passed. Conversations died whenever he drew near. A few kids smiled nervously. But a larger number scowled at the infamous traitor who had turned 'their' xeno over to the Feds.

No matter that most of the students only heard of it when the news broke on Friday. Not even the latest reports — about improvements in the star-visitor's health and progress in crossing the language divide — seemed to make much difference in the mood on campus. The alien had become part of the greater world, and this place was again just another drab American high school.

It got worse indoors. Soon he couldn't take more than a dozen paces without hearing someone *horking* in the back of their throat, as if preparing to spit. It became a theme song, following him around. When Mark reached his locker and spied a greasy brown fluid leaking out the bottom, he decided not to bother opening it, denying any satisfaction to those who were watching.

A crowd had gathered at the door to history class. Any hope of slipping inside and quietly taking his seat was dashed when yet another news crew emerged from the room, pushed by an affably insistent Mr. Castro, wearing his typical striped shirt and colorful tie. Hot camera lights made beads of sweat shimmer on his peaked, receding hairline.

"Enough please! We're serious students and educators here. Save your questions for off-hours. Anyway, I was just a witness. The real heroes ..."

Mark tried to melt into the crowd, but Mr. Castro spotted him first.

"Well, speak of the young man himself. Here's Mark Bamford, the fellow who invited me to participate in last Thursday's adventure."

Mark winced when he saw the camera crew was from Channel Ten, one of the local stations that missed out on the 'adventure' when they refused his invitation, dismissing him as a crank. A costly mistake, and now they seemed eager to take revenge by painting Mark in the worst possible light, making up ridiculous motives.

That he hoped for a reward from the government.

That he was taking revenge for a romantic disappointment.

That he had religious objections to aliens.

That he was already talking to Hollywood agents (a few *had* left messages — Mark didn't plan on answering) about doing his story as a mini-series.

None of the reporters told anything like the true story of those frantic hours that he and Alex spent — that nervous Thursday evening — setting things up just right. They had to act fast. Scott Tepper and Tom Spencer — leading their strange jock-nerd alliance — were already gathering a caravan of private vehicles, preparing to transport the xeno off to some hip refuge deep inside the L.A. sprawl, rationalizing to themselves that they were doing *something heroic,* defending a 'guest' from the vile-distrusted government.

Oh, it would have been easy enough just to foil their crazy plan. If that was all Mark and Alex wanted, they only had to phone up the Air Force. Or Cirocco labs.

But that option raised worries of its own. Did it make sense to transfer custody of the castaway from one group of secretive paranoids to another? Tom Spencer had a point. Some clique of bureaucratic poobahs would surely talk themselves into thinking just like Scott and Gornet! Foolishly trying to hide all evidence of an extraterrestrial encounter, keeping the news to an elite in-group, and coming up with elaborate reasons to justify it to themselves.

The world has plenty of bright fools in it, eager to act out movie clichés.

Oh, the secret probably wouldn't hold for very long, for any group. Mark doubted that any cover story could last in today's world. Take the crazy notion that three generations of top savants had been studying a spacecraft that crashed at Roswell, New Mexico, ever since 1949.

Right. Hundreds of scientists and engineers, investigating fantastic alien technologies — with none of them blabbing in all that time? Not even when they retired? Nobody who actually knew a living, breathing scientist would believe such nonsense. The best minds are independent; the very trait that made them "best." Even a military man like Dad would eventually get fed up with secrecy that stretched on and on, for no apparent reason. Especially if it appeared also to violate the law.

And nowadays, secrets can leak, 'accidentally', by as many paths as there are addresses on the internet.

Still, some group of adult Gornets might decide to try. In fact, given human nature, they probably would.

So, for two wild hours, Mark and Alex made calls and pounded on doors, collecting half a dozen reputable witnesses, then driving around — with several of them fuming impatiently — till the moment seemed right to dial up Cirocco.

As he elbowed his way into the classroom, ignoring Channel Ten's shouted questions, Mark found himself almost wishing he never made that call — even though the plan worked better than he or Alex could have hoped.

IT TOOK Mr. Castro ten minutes to get rid of the TV people — maybe he wasn't trying all that hard — and to settle class back to any semblance of a normal routine, taking roll and collecting the weekend's essay assignment about the European Thirty Years War.

The teacher shook his head at the skimpy pile. Mark's contribution amounted to just two pages, rehashed from a single Wikipedia article. In big type, with generous margins.

"Now people," Mr. Castro said. "I know there have been some distractions lately, but that's no excuse for slacking off. In fact, this startling news about First Contact ought to emphasize the need for *focus*. What event could possibly make clearer the importance of education for your future?"

A hand shot up from the forward right. Dave McCarty, wearing his usual black leather jacket, spoke without waiting to be called.

"Why?" he asked, pushing contemptuously at the textbook in front of him. "Everything we know is obsolete! All our technology, science, arts ... every bit of it is passé. In a few years we'll be using teleportation and warp drives, learning whatever we want from pills!"

That drew laughter. But some classmates also nodded.

"So," Mr. Castro asked. "Should we dismiss our old-fashioned schools till then?"

"Sure! Why waste brain cells studying stuff we'll never need?"

"Even the history of your species and civilization?"

"*Especially* history. It's irrelevant. Everything up until now will be remembered as a time of primitives, like cavemen. B.C. ... for Before Contact!" McCarty chortled, clearly believing he was on a roll.

"And do the rest of you feel the same way? Or the opposite?"

Silence. Mark, especially, didn't want to attract any more attention. Anyway, he wasn't sure he disagreed with Dave.

Mr. Castro walked around the desk and put his hand on an Earth globe that always stood there.

"I'll grant you, it seems like a pretty small place in a big universe right now," he mused. "Though our ancestors thought it was vast and filled with dark unknowns." He set the globe spinning. "Take for example the period we've been studying, the Sixteenth and Seventeenth Centuries —"

Students groaned. This teacher would use any excuse to swerve back on course.

"— a time of wrenching transition, perhaps even more shattering than the one we are about to enter."

Froggi Hayashi snorted from a seat in back.

"How could anything compare with *first contact?* To meet powerful aliens with incredible technologies you don't understand —"

"Exactly!" Mr. Castro grinned. And he waited. One of his famous pauses. Which usually meant that something — some connection — had been made. One that should be obvious to anyone who was paying attention.

Amid the ensuing hush, Mark felt a sudden wrench of understanding.

Oh, he thought.

Almost against his will, Mark's hand started to raise ... but another voice spoke up first.

"People in Africa ... and Asia and the Americas ... that was when *they* had to adapt to strange new things — to *aliens* and their technologies — when they faced European invaders."

Mark turned around to see Helene Shockley, sitting to his left and two chairs back. As usual, she was simply overwhelming, with black hair falling in ringlets over dusky shoulders. To Mark's surprise — especially after the events of Thursday night — she glanced his way with a fleeting smile that sent his heart lurching in his chest.

"Good point," Mr. Castro answered with a nod. "And there's no question that those Europeans were outright invaders in the Americas. There, the newcomers — or aliens, if you will — swarmed in without mercy, taking whatever they wanted, by force. They also brought waves of horrible disease that caught native peoples in the Western Hemisphere unprepared ... something that I hope our leaders are bearing in mind right now."

Several students blanched at the idea. Mark recalled how close he and his friends had been to the alien, breathing the same air! A plague from the stars. Now wouldn't that just round out the whole month?

"Elsewhere, things were more complicated. Especially for the first couple of centuries after da Gama's voyage, when Europeans came to Asia and Africa more as traders than conquerors, and where disease was much less of a factor. Even there, however, the arrival of a foreign culture and new technologies had profound effects, disrupting everything that had been static and assumed in local cultures. Even powerful nations that tried to control the effects of contact, like China and Japan, wound up destabilized, plunging into devastating internal strife.

"Still, none of those conflicts would match the bitter clash we've been studying for the last week, an awful conflagration that wracked Europe itself during the very same period."

This time, the groan from Dave and some others held a tone of grudging admiration for the smooth way the teacher segued discussion back into the syllabus. Mr. Castro swiveled toward a map that hung from the south wall, covered with arrows showing the harsh, back-and-forth struggle called the Thirty Years War.

"Can anyone explain why this period was even more riotous *inside* Europe than in far-off lands that their ships were surprising and exploiting?"

Trembling a little, Arlene Hsu raised her hand.

"B-because of the ... Protestant Reformation?"

Mr. Castro always took a gentler tone when answering Arlene. It obviously took courage for her to speak up. Freewheeling class discussions hadn't been the style in school where she came from — a small town north of Guangdong.

"Yes, that was the reason given by kings and princes and city states for waging brutal war on their neighbors. A dispute over religious doctrine. But does that completely explain it? Anybody."

Forgetting his vow to stay silent, Mark raised a hand.

"Weren't they just as shook up by ... by all this new *contact* with outsiders, as anybody else was?"

Mr. Castro smiled. Mark hoped it wasn't too obvious that the teacher felt grateful for being chosen as one of the Thursday night witnesses. He had clearly enjoyed the chance to participate, helping to transfer the alien into professional hands while also preventing any government cover-up ... and getting to watch history happen in real-time.

Fine, but Mark didn't need 'teacher's pet' added to the things murmured behind his back.

"You may be onto something, Mr. Bamford. Their world *was* changing. Can anybody suggest what could have shaken up Europe, at this time?"

Hands raised. One student after another started contributing to a growing list.

"New weapons. New war tactics."

"All the gold and silver and stuff stolen from Mexico. That would've changed the economy."

"There were new crops too ... like corn? Potatoes and tobacco?"

"New *ideas* —"

"— spread by printing presses. Didn't all this happen just a little after that German guy, Gutberg —"

"Gutenberg."

"— yeah. Suddenly books and newspapers were cheap."

"And new ideas don't always bring folks together, do they? Sometimes they frighten people, or divide them. In the beginning, printing was more effective at spreading hate than encouraging tolerance. It took many generations to change that. Anything else?"

"How about dangerous ideas that came *from* those places the ships went?" Arlene asked, and Mr. Castro nodded.

"Interesting point, Miss Hsu! Did cultural colonization go both ways, affecting the invaders as much as the invaded? That's not often talked about. Maybe you could do a paper."

Again, groans. Before the bell, several more research topics were sure to be assigned.

"How about —" Mark heard Helene say behind him, her voice more hushed than usual. "How about the very fact that the world was bigger ... a much bigger place, after Columbus? Maybe that changed view kind of drove them all a bit ... crazy?"

There was silence for several heartbeats after that, as each student let the implication sink in. How her words applied today. Even Mr. Castro appeared subdued.

Anyway, the point was made. Even Dave McCarty clearly realized it. History still had a place in the post-Contact world.

"Excellent, Helene. That would also make a really interesting topic for a —"

Mr. Castro halted when the door creaked open. A student carrying a hall pass entered, handing the teacher a slip of paper. He read it with a pursed brow.

"Bamford," he said at last, holding the slip out to Mark. "You're wanted in the main office."

Mark stood, lifting his backpack. He didn't dare look around to see how others took this — yet another sign of special treatment. But at least now he might escape new assignments.

"Check my web site," the teacher said as he departed, dashing even that silver lining. "Tonight's homework will be a thirty minute e-debate, at the usual time. You can take first chair in the argument *against* contact, Mark. We'll decide the exact topic while you're away."

Mark tried not to wince, especially with Helene watching. *I guess it wouldn't do for Castro to show gratitude, for my inviting him to help make history for a change, instead of just teaching it.*

The halls felt eerily empty with all students in class. Along with his footsteps, faint echoes carried indoors from the athletic field, where coaches hollered at the lazy as they had for generations, probably going all the way back to Sparta. Mark shuffled along toward the administration suites, wondering *now what?*

It must be about Xeno.

Sure enough, when he entered the outer Administration Office Alex was already present. So was Barry Tang. They all shared a silent nod as the secretary ushered them through a final door into the sanctum of Principal Jeffers.

Jeffers cut an imposing figure. Almost two meters tall, he had actually trained for six weeks with the San Francisco Forty-Niners before failing to make the final roster. That was many years ago, but he still kept the jersey from his brief pro career in a glass case, next to photos from his time as a Peace Corps volunteer. The principal believed that everyone should have a broad range of interests.

"Here they are," he said in a deep voice as the students came in. Two other adults turned at the same time, causing Mark to stumble briefly in surprise. One of them was a Marine Corps officer — his father!

The other, a pale-haired woman wearing a lab coat, smiled as Alexandra Behr blurted — "Mom! What are you doing here?"

Dad shared a silent look with Mark, saying *wait and see.*

"We're still looking for Barry's folks," Principal Jeffers said. "I can't let him go on a field trip without their permission. So if you're really in a hurry..."

"We are, I'm afraid," Major Bamford said. "We'll just have to take Alex and Mark for now, and hope Barry can follow."

Alex blinked.

"Field trip?"

Mark's father drew a folded sheet of paper from his tunic pocket. It had official-looking seals and signatures — plus some odd-shaped blotchy symbols on the bottom.

"Not a normal one, by any means," he said. "It seems you've been invited."

"Invited?"

This time it was Mark's turn to express puzzlement. So Major Bamford explained.

"For a reunion. With the visitor. We're going to see your strange little man from the stars."

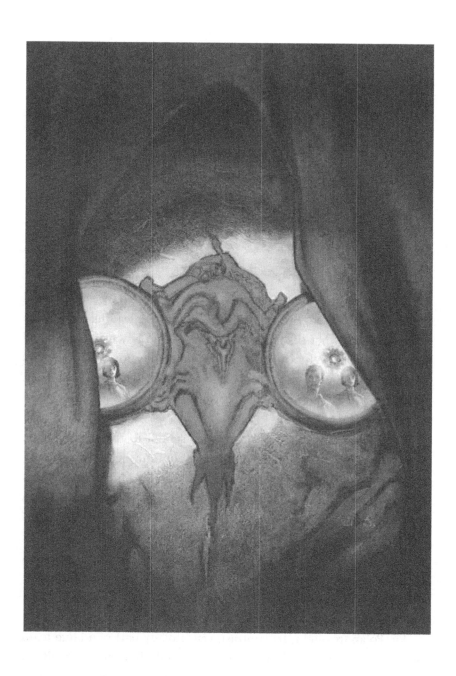

4

INDIVIDUAL TUTORING

Barry was devastated of course. He wheedled and complained. But nothing – none of his pleading assurances about what his folks *would* say — had any effect. Principal Jeffers was firm. When it came to responsibility for a minor, rules were rules. No parent-signed permission slip? Then no exit from school grounds before the bell. Period. It would be just Mark and Alex plus one parent each.

Piloting everybody in his car, from school to the nearby base, Major Bamford seemed to have added about four inches to his chest, all of it pride. As he commented to Dr. Karen Polandres-Behr, Alex's mother, "I've taken Mark around the world with me and shown him some amazing things. But now he's outdone all that in just a few days."

In other words, Dad knew that his own clearance and technical slot – as high as they were — wouldn't normally let him anywhere near the alien. He was getting in today solely as Mark's guardian and escort. Grinning, he didn't seem to mind at all.

Dr. Polandres-Behr, by contrast, was already part of a large team that had been assembled to see to Xeno's needs. But she kept taciturn about details. Though scientists from many nations were now involved, and an international committee had been appointed to keep an eye on things, this remained mostly a U. S. government operation. Information would be released through channels in an 'orderly manner.'

Major Bamford had to brake hard at Melrose, giving way to a swarm of dark-clad men and women on great big motorcycles, who refused to have their band separated by something as trivial as a traffic signal. Mark saw the badges of at least seven big, national motorcycle clubs, emblazoned across scores of denim and leather jackets and the air fumed with smoke from gas-powered Harley bikes ... electrics might be faster, sure, but no sissy here.

Dad muttered something low... then again as a mob of pedestrians undulated past, attired far more brightly, in colored dashikis and muumuus and Hawaiian shirts, with wide-brimmed hats to ward off the desert sun. About half of them were shaking rattles or tambourines, as they undulated toward the Base.

Mark had never seen traffic like this in sleepy little Twenty-Nine Palms. Every hotel was full, bought out by news organizations and special interest groups. The RV parks overflowed and nearby Joshua Tree Park had transformed into a forest of tents, many of them without permits. The empty zone outside the Marine Corps gate was now crammed with gawkers and demonstrators waving signs.

Overall, the mood seemed decent enough. Mostly hopeful and festive. Though some of the signs, especially along the last hundred meters or so, took on a darker tone. From demanding to downright hostile.

Ask The Alien About God!
Beam Me Off This Rock!
Sell Our Rockrap Stars: GET CURES FOR CANCER
Alien cuisine: I'll buy a franchise!
SHOW US THE ONES WHO CRASHED *EARLIER!*
Make the Xeno Tell Us About D.E.R.P!

"What the heck does that one even *mean?*" asked Dad, gesturing at the last placard. Mark shrugged, not bothering to explain. Alex pointed to some signs that only bore strange smudges of dots on them.

"I heard about those. You point your phone..." she aimed her pen-cell, using it like a telescope. "The image deconvolves into a whole augmented reality display. Wow!" A puzzled look crossed her face, then she grinned. "It turns Twenty-Nine Palms into some kind of alien seascape! Like the whole town is underwater."

Dang. Girls who can use words like 'deconvolves.' She spends way too much time around Barry.

Mark was tempted to dig into his pocket and pull out the Tru Vu specs. The reporters from Channel Ten had never asked for them back. They were so grateful for the news-scoop, that night, they probably would have given him half the contents of their mobile van and half of next year's budget! If he put them on, and glanced at that code placard out there, presumably he'd see what Alex was peering at with her pen, only in full sensurround. But he felt sheepish about showing it to Dad. The prim Marine would probably make him give the specs back, no matter how much he had earned them.

At last, they reached the main gate. A brief show of ID cards let them past the first checkpoint onto the base, whereupon traffic cleared up considerably. They drove by barracks, offices and the Post Exchange before reaching a second guard post near the big airfield. Here a second inspection was more rigorous. Each of them had to get out of the car to face everything from sniff-dogs to sophisticated scanners, while the vehicle itself got a thorough going-over.

When that scrutinizing finished, they drove past the flight control tower and alongside a long runway. The howl of engines went bone-deep. A steady flow of fighters overhead escorted heavy transports as three of the heavier planes touched down, one after another, bringing experts and equipment from all over the globe.

Major Bamford bore left toward a cluster of buildings that stood at the far end, offset from anything else, bordering only a vast expanse of desert, dotted with spiky Joshua trees.

A pair of old hangars had been hastily augmented with several white, inflatable structures. Dr. Polandres-Behr explained that nearby trailers supplied air conditioning and environmental services. Vans came and went as Mark watched people in lab whites emerge through tunnels equipped with triple doors.

Airlocks, he realized, recalling how Mr. Castro had described the awful effects of 'alien' diseases on native populations, here on this very continent, just half a millennium ago.

Maybe I wasn't invited after all. Could this be just an excuse to get me into quarantine? Because I was exposed —

But that didn't make sense. The same thing could have been accomplished during the weekend. And he would have been quick to cooperate.

A blonde lieutenant met them at the entrance to the biggest inflated structure, checking their identifications on an electronic clipboard. She accepted Mark's California driver's license, confirming its coded information, but then frowned over Alex's learner's permit — not exactly a *secure credential.* Well, anyone could tell she was barely sixteen. How much threat did they expect from a kid!

(Well, okay, a kid with a second-degree black belt, who could scurry up rock walls like a spider. And say words like "deconvolve," for heck-sake.)

Finally, something flashed on the lieutenant's smart clipboard and she stepped aside. "Please suit up. Coveralls and booties. Don't put on gloves or masks unless you're asked to by your guide."

Dr. Polandres-Behr smiled and explained as they entered.

"We're still taking precautions, though by now we're pretty sure the chance of cross-infection is minimal."

Deeply relieved, Mark passed through a sealed pathway. It felt like walking in a long, slender bubble. Their group passed two more sets of hissing irises before entering a large chamber where slick-textured dungarees hung from hooks along one wall. Dr. Polandres-Behr helped them put on slipperlike shoe-covers and snug caps, leaving only their hands and faces exposed.

"We have a filtered laminar airflow system. Nobody wears masks anymore unless they get real close. It looks as if the Garubis' microbial parasites don't have a clue how to attack Earthling body cells, and vice versa."

"Garubis?"

Dr. Polandres-Behr glanced at Mark.

"Oh, that's right. You haven't heard. It's all coming out in a press conference, this evening. The news couldn't be more exciting." She smiled and suddenly Mark glimpsed what Alex might look like, when she grew up a little more. If her luck held.

"First, we know their species name. They are called *Garubis*. And there's more. Helped by a worldwide network of experts with high-speed computers ... and some gifted amateurs who joined in via the web ... we've managed to crack the language barrier."

"So fast!" Alex said, beaming at her mother. "That seems impossible."

"He helped us." Dr. Polandres-Behr gestured ahead of them, toward the next enclosure they were now approaching. "In fact, that's why you two kids were invited here today."

"Um," Mark nodded. "Invited?"

The word still sounded improbable.

"That's right. It was almost the first thing Na-bistaka asked for, once we started communicating. He wanted to see the kids who rescued him."

It was almost too much to take in at once. *Na-bistaka,* the xeno's name. And the word — 'rescued.'

Mark suddenly realized that a knot of tension had been coiled inside of him for days, worrying about that. *Had* he and Alex really done the right thing? No matter what was said by the students at TNPHS — or adults, or the news media or government officials — only one entity had the right to decide.

He understood part of the reason when they rounded the next corner and saw the alien's new accommodations.

Good-bye kennel cage, hello Plaza Hotel!

Well, that might overstate the difference. It was still an enclosure and the 'visitor' wasn't exactly free to depart and enjoy every nearby tourist spot. But the glass panels had curtains on the inside, which evidently could be closed whenever the occupant chose.

Within, a kind of *nest* had been created on top of a four-poster bed, using strips of fabric. Nearby, some small tables and chairs must have come from a children's furniture store. Mark spotted a refrigerator, a microwave oven and a food processor, arrayed in a half-sized kitchenette ... plus a stainless steel bucket with a spring lid that had sticky, grayish-red dribbles down one side. He shuddered, knowing what that was for.

This strange creature can cross the gulf of stars. But doesn't bother to maintain cleanliness in its own living space?

One end of the room was jammed with top quality audio-visual and computer equipment — six or seven giant flat-screens and a pixelated wall — while a trestle table lay strewn with all kinds of objects, from books to dolls to construction toys. Three humans stood near a second table wearing gauze masks, but these had been pulled down to let them speak more freely. One fellow tapped excitedly on a big display that showed bright pinpoints, annotated with letters and numbers.

A star chart, Mark realized. Another person huddled over some kind of technical schematic, shaking her head.

All of that was peripheral, of course. The center of attention could only be a short figure on the left, standing next to the second scientist, wearing a hooded silk bathrobe — bright scarlet — that dragged on the floor, preventing any view of the wearer's body. Mark did hear a voice, though — the same *chuttering* sound that he remembered from that brief encounter in Colin Gornet's cabaña.

Soon, an amplified computer translation echoed from nearby speakers.

"No. No. No. Your electronic devices will not deliver the degrees of modulation necessary to create a quantum tunneling effect. It appears that I shall have to use up yet another of my precious emergency storage units, in order to recall the design parameters and draw them for you."

The computer-generated translation conveyed a tone of resignation, plus something else. Was Mark just imagining *disdain* in the flat, toneless words? Well, a brainy alien envoy might well be entitled to feel some of that, stuck down here with cavemen.

"Wow," commented Alexandra.

Her mother agreed with an emphatic nod. "Wow is right! I've been away just a few hours, and yet the level of syntactical abstraction has improved remarkably, along with grammatical construction. Those self-correcting language algorithms from Carnegie-Mellon are just fantastic!"

Alex shook her head.

"No, I mean wow ... he's teaching us how to make a machine that can do *quantum tunneling?* I thought that was just in Star Trek."

Then she blinked a couple of times and glanced at Mark, who nodded back.

We are in Star Trek. Or something scarier. Either way, it sure ain't Kansas.

"What's the objective?" Major Bamford asked, standing on his toes to peer at the schematics. If they were secret, they had no business being out in the open like this. "What are you trying to build?"

Not a spacecraft or transport, Mark realized. The design looked way too simple, no fuselage or flight surfaces. No place for a passenger. Anyway, he doubted that *Na-bistaka* needed something like that right now.

"A radio," he guessed.

Dr. Polandres-Behr nodded. "That's right, Mark. Just as soon as we could talk to each other, Na-bistaka started teaching us how to help him to ... well ... phone home."

She shrugged at using the obvious cliché. And for a moment there seemed little to say. Not until Major Bamford asked.

"Are we going to do that? Yell for his friends to come get him?"

"Good question. It's a matter for debate ... for the whole world to discuss. And after tonight, the discussion will be wide open. Nobody should be excluded.

"Obviously, there are ramifications. Right now, there's still a chance to limit this contact — though at some moral cost. But once we've sent Na-bistaka's message ..."

She let the implications hang, for each person to finish in his or her own mind.

Once we've sent it, everything that we talked about this morning in Mr. Castro's class will begin, Mark knew. We'll enter a time of struggle and change. One in which we're the primitives, underdogs struggling to catch up. Even if the aliens prove to be as nice as can be ... there will be challenges and pain. More than any of us can imagine.

Mark couldn't help feeling a little guilty about that.

He thought about those native Mexican tribes who allied themselves with Hernán Cortés, helping him conquer the hated Aztecs. Would those allies have treated the Spaniards so well, if they had an inkling about what would come next?

Should we help this creature? Or hide him somewhere deep and hope his friends never show up asking about him? Maybe Scott Tepper's plan would have been better after all ... a brief celebrity curiosity, that then vanished into legend.

Mark felt guilty for thinking that, too.

"So, do we get anything in exchange for helping?" Major Bamford asked. Dad was always the pragmatist — and the eternal optimist — of the family.

"Good question. We're studying the capsule he arrived in. It seems to be just a life raft, lacking any of the really juicy technologies for interstellar flight. Still, the circuits and things he's teaching us to build for the communication device may help us understand some key principles. As for any formal *quid pro quo?* We haven't raised the issue of trade or compensation. It seemed ... premature."

Mark wondered what he would ask for, if the occasion ever came up. Then he realized, it might be very close.

Let's say he suddenly offers me three wishes. What'll I ask for?

Yeah, a dumb thought. But he found that his brain wasn't working too well. In fact, it felt like mush.

The scarlet dressing gown abruptly straightened, rising a little taller, as if the wearer sensed something. The hooded figure turned slowly, until a pair of bulbous, golden eyes appeared, set weirdly on both sides of a slender snout. The alien face — even more unnerving than it had been in poor lighting — seemed to change as its gaze settled on Mark and Alex. Somehow, it conveyed recognition.

He knows us.

Abandoning the technician and schematics, Na-bistaka moved closer, facing the glass partition and dropping onto a pile of cushions. One gnarly hand lifted, raising a floppy sleeve, to point at Mark and his friend. More chuttering sounds emerged.

"You came." said a wall speaker, conveying the computer translation. *"In studying your primitive data stores, I found it culturally problematic whether larval humans would be allowed to attend me, even at my direct request. Does this mean you have advanced? Have you been promoted, because of your actions, to adult status?"*

Mark glanced at Alex, recalling her learner's permit, and thought about his own steep car insurance rates. And poor Barry, who could not come at all, because of the school district's absurdly overprotective rules.

"Um ... I don't think so. We're here with our parents."

The golden eyes rotated independently — an eerie sight — to examine Major Bamford and Dr. Polandres-Behr.

"Superintended contact with an outsider. Consistent with low reproductive rates and high nurturing emphasis. Yet, from direct experience I know that the late-larval form is allowed to form undisciplined and unsupervised cultural association units.

"Moreover, these pseudo-tribal units may freely conspire against the interests of the common good! Is this a common pattern?"

This time, Mark had to think hard. Na-bistaka was talking about high school, about the cliques that form among teens ... and about how some of them recently got carried away with their own sense of drama and rebellion, attempting to handle a major event — one with implications for all humanity — completely by themselves.

"It happens," Alex answered. "Kids today have more freedom to experiment. Maybe too much. Or too little. There's a lot of arguments."

The alien castaway's snout opened and closed a few times.

"Argument seems endemic to the peculiar culture that produces the most

noise on this planet. One that is rife with mutual suspicion and recrimina-tion. Disorganization and abandonment of tradition. These things I attempted to study from afar, before the malfunction."

Mark squelched a temptation to feel insulted. After all, Na-bistaka wasn't saying anything new about contemporary American life. The *noise* he must have been analyzing from some cloaked perch in space came from Earth's electronic media. The 'malfunction' was presumably what led to him becoming stranded in the California desert, to be picked up by undisciplined larval humans.

"Argument can be a good thing," Alex suggested, never shy, step-ping closer to the glass barrier. "It's how we negotiate. Point out each others' mistakes and learn from our *own* mistakes when others point them out to us. Even mistakes that were ... well ... part of tradition."

The bulby eyes seemed to glitter. The alien gabbled a bit in its own tongue, before the mechanical voice translated.

"So? Larval humans may question ancestral tribal wisdom? Based on what qualifications? What expertise?"

Alex blinked a couple of times.

"No ... qualifications. I guess we're encouraged to do it ... for prac-tice?" You could see her confidence ebb, as she spoke. "To ... to become better at it?"

Na-bistaka never seemed to blink at all. The steady stare made Mark uncomfortable. Especially when one of the eyes turned to fix on him.

"To become better at disloyalty? Then why did you abandon that goal, and hand me over to authorities?"

Evidently, it was Mark's turn. Visibly shaken, Alex seemed grateful for the chance to step back. Mark had no patience for theory. He went for the simplest answer.

"It seemed to us that ... well, your life was in danger!"

Mark felt Dad's hand on his shoulder. It came as both a comfort and an irritation. But he could not bring himself to shrug it off.

"Duly noted. This explains much. Suggests much," commented the Garubis castaway. *"I shall adjust my prognosis. My recommendation."*

Silence held, on both sides of the barrier. Alex swallowed, clearly shaken. Neither of the kids had come here expecting that their words might affect anything. The word *recommendation* sounded ominous.

"Well," Mark ventured. "I'm glad things turned out all right."

That brought a strange sound from the creature within the enclosure.

"Have they?"

Mark blinked.

"What?"

"Have they turned out all right?"

Somehow, the computerized translation sounded bemused. Ironic.

"Certainly my own position was improved by your intervention, trans-ferring my custody to more responsible parties. You personally acted to divert destiny onto a fresh path, one with unforeseen future outcomes."

Mark wasn't sure he liked the sound of that, in keeping with all of Na-bistaka's statement's so far. He swallowed, unable to think of anything to say.

"What do you mean?" Alexandra asked. Once again the alien stepped forward to the glass that separated it from the young humans.

"I mean that there will now be consequences.

"All actions have them.

"Are you prepared to reap what you have sown?"

5

CLASS DISCUSSION

The planet called Earth launched into its first-ever universal conversation.

At one level or another, a majority of its eight billion inhabitants took part — some through electronic forums and scientifically tabulated opinion polls, while countless others participated through the babble of rumor and argument in teahouses, marketplaces and teeming bazaars. News and debate trickled down via mass media while public perceptions percolated upward, even in dictatorships. Local officials asked hairdressers, taxi drivers and bartenders what people were saying, then passed word to mayors, then governors and so on. But mostly, it happened online, in a million soshsites, bitcafes, eposcenes and blags.

The Great Discussion was ardent. Opinionated. Boulevards filled with mass demonstrations. Here and there, fevered emotions broke into riots. Some buildings and effigies burned ...

... and yet, for the most part — to the surprise of nearly everyone — the debate was rather earnest. This issue seemed to go beyond nationalism or politics. It was just too important for most people to leave to passion.

Shall we transmit a message?

That was the central question, solemnly argued from back alleys in Dacca to the yacht basins of Sydney, from impoverished hovels in Quito, where the TV was the only source of illumination, to penthouse apartments in Helsinki.

Shall we send the xeno-guest's call for help?

If it were simply a matter of beaming a radio bulletin to space, there would be no point even raising the issue. All sorts of nations, cities and even private individuals owned high power transmitters. Even if the world reached a 99% agreement to stay quiet, *somebody* would surely disagree and defy mass opinion by shouting to the stars. Today, more than ever, it was the human way.

But it seemed that new and sophisticated technologies were needed, in order to send an SOS bulletin to the nearest Garubis outpost in time to do any good. For now and the immediate future, only the U.S. government had a clue how to build such machinery.

In theory, the United Nations Supervisory Committee could insist that those blueprints be posted on the internet. But they had no intention of doing that right now. Perhaps not ever.

It all hung on what the *world consensus* decided — if agreement proved possible at all. For weeks, it did not seem to be.

MEANWHILE, for Mark Bamford, it was back to the grind. Back to high school — the modern form of incarceration for those found guilty of being young.

In some other era, a sturdy fellow who was just about to turn seventeen might be a confident hunter, already at the top of his skill, faster and more daring than anyone else in the band. As a farmer, he would have fields to plow and probably a family to feed. In ancient kingdoms like Rome or Babylon, a fellow his age might by now have scars from a soldier's battles. And he would know how to make nearly all his own tools.

Even until a few decades ago, if you were eager to escape high school, you could always drop out and enlist.

No longer. Nowadays, even the army wouldn't take you without a diploma. So, you might as well just stick it out, get grades, go to college. Sure, nobody would take you seriously there, either; but at least college was more interesting and fun. You'd finally get an adult's freedom — without the responsibilities ... or any of the respect. Till graduation, then, life was on hold however you looked at it. Just one thought made the prospect bearable.

Everybody has to go through this.

It's just my turn.

Only now that wasn't exactly true, was it? The news cameras had vanished from Twenty-Nine Palms High within a week after that fateful Thursday. Yet, so long as the whole world was transfixed on the issue of first contact, Mark's position at school settled into a rhythm of grueling discomfort.

It wasn't all sullen silence. In fact, more students spoke to him now than before all this started, perhaps out of some vain hope of being invited to meet the Xeno. But soon most realized Mark had no back door pass. That one encounter at the base had been pretty much it.

Even Gornet's pals stopped following him around with *horking* sounds. They still glowered, and Mark felt certain they would have pounced by now, pummeling him after school — except that it seemed pointless.

I have a reputation as a tattler, he realized. *They won't beat me up because they think I'd squeal.*

He wouldn't! Not over a simple bruising. He wanted to tell them that. Get it over with, dammit! The guerrillitas near Caracas had been far more frightening than some putzy gang of SoCal teen-athletes. Anyway, they might be surprised how many licks of his own he got in.

But Mark kept his mouth shut. Anything he said now would just be used for mockery.

He stopped using his locker. Every time Alex Behr and Conner Mills accompanied him to practice at the climbing wall, Mark carefully checked the ropes. Once, he found a few suspicious nicks, which he repaired without comment. Beyond that, the goal was to endure till summer. *Then just one more year,* he told himself.

Another week passed, and then another while the world bickered over the Message Proposal. Then one day, trucks arrived and parked next to the athletic field, disgorging a motley array of carnies and roustabouts who got to work, gradually setting up tents and rides for the Twenty-Nine Palms Desert Carnival, which always coincided with the high school's Homecoming Dance.

Mark winced when he saw banners announcing this year's theme — an alien motif — silvery UFO types, still more popular in the public mind than the weirdly realistic Garubis image. There was even talk of changing the school mascot from a cartoony spy to E.T.

Agh, he thought, wishing Dad would just get promoted or transferred again. But as the crank callers and drive-by vandals ebbed away, Major Bamford returned to his squadron, now in the thick of testing new "gimmicks" using bits of alien technology. In fact, Mark hadn't seen Dad so happy since before Mom died.

I might be too, if I had something useful to do.

Even history class was no escape. Mr. Castro finally gave up trying to focus on the past. Now, every discussion had something to do with the great big international debate over The Message.

TODAY'S CLASS focused on the surprise announcement by an ecumenical conclave of religious leaders, ranging from the Pope and Dalai Lama to Jewish, Muslim, Mormon and Hindu scholars.

Morally, we must transmit the Visitor's call for help, stated the joint declaration. *Whether these beings prove beneficent or hostile, it is vital that we begin relations with a righteous act. We must, all of us together, put our trust in the wisdom and mercy of God.*

This communiqué had profound effects worldwide, even on non-believers. Never before had a single choice been portrayed in the same moral terms by all major faiths at the same time. Some of

Mark's fellow students were also influenced to change their minds. But not Dave McCarty.

"It's all propaganda," he muttered. "The priests have had the masses in their grip for centuries. Since before there was writing! Now they're doing it again."

Arlene Hsu shook her head. She had grown more confident during the last two months, exchanging ideas informally, with increasing boldness and often free-of-facts, in the American style.

"How can you say they are insincere, Dave! Contact with a huge and powerful alien culture will bring in new ideas, challenging all of the old faiths. Why should the religious leaders want competition —"

"Because they're confident they'll win out, of course. I bet they see a chance to grab converts among the stars! Or maybe they just believe their own propaganda."

Mr. Castro stepped around to sit on the front of his desk.

"You use that word pretty freely, Dave. Do you have a clear idea what it means?"

"What? Propaganda?" McCarty blinked a couple of times. It was one of those terms you just grew up using, without ever seeing it defined.

"Propaganda ... is where the folks with power or money or influence —"

"— elites —"

"Yeah, elites want the masses to believe something that'll help keep 'em under control, doing what the masters want. In olden times they did it by preaching 'obey the kings and priests.' They did it in temples and churches and when they hired guys like Homer to chant songs about heroes and gods ..."

"And nowadays they do it with television, movies, commercials." Froggi Hayashi interrupted, with a nod to his friend.

"... and *schools*." Dave finished. That triggered agreeing laughter from several students.

"So," Mr. Castro concluded, tapping his own chest. "That makes me a tool of the establishment, cramming conformity messages into young minds, molding them into compliant little villagers."

"And consumers!" interjected Paulina Isfahani. "Got to keep the economy churning, after all."

The teacher sighed. "Ah, it's sad. You're all too young to be so cynical."

That won the teacher a flurry of groans that he tolerated with a grin.

"And yet, I wonder — could that be a clue?"

The remark drew puzzled looks.

"You mean the fact *that* we're cynical?" asked Helene Shockley from behind Mark. He didn't have to turn around; Mark knew exactly what she wore today — a turquoise top with beaded trim and a plunging neckline that stopped just short of breaking the school's liberal dress code.

"What could our cynicism be a clue to, Mr. Castro?" Helene finished.

"Why, a clue to *which* propaganda messages we should be watching out for, of course. You all seem to agree that indoctrination fills the airwaves, newspapers, movies — and schools," he conceded with a nod to Dave. "Persuasive messages that are nevertheless too subtle to be noticed by the common man or woman on the street. Right?"

Nods of agreement all around.

"But *you* are all capable of noticing, and rising above this pervasive brainwashing. Is that it?"

More nods, though not quite as quick or vigorous as before. *Uh-oh*, Mark thought, sensing one of the teacher's trademark logical traps.

"Well, well. How fortunate I am that you seventeen-year-old juniors and seniors in *my* history class happen to be so much smarter and more observant than all those sheep out there! All the doctors and lawyers and mechanics and such — *they* can't resist the brainwashing, but you have. How do you account for this amazing statistical fluke? Anybody?"

Now there was stone silence, until Arlene raised her hand again.

"Everybody likes to think they are smart, I guess ... and that everyone else is clueless."

Mr. Castro nodded.

"Some of you, at university, will study scientific method and learn how easily we're fooled by what we want to believe. You'll be sent out to survey people on the street, asking two questions. *How did you arrive at your own set of beliefs? And why do your opponents believe what they do?*

"Can anyone guess what nearly always happens?"

"Um ... isn't it obvious?" Mark ventured. "People say they got their *own* beliefs by calmly looking at the evidence."

"Right. And this crosses all boundaries of politics or culture. Left or right or whatever. We ascribe our own opinions to *logical appraisal of the situation and the facts,* while we think that our enemies believe what they do because of malice, or greed, or gullibility, or else flaws in their character."

Helene mulled this over, then commented. "I guess that's human nature. We come up with reasons to think well of ourselves, and put down those we don't like. It makes their opinions seem less important. Especially when they don't like us."

This time, Mark turned around in time to catch Helene looking briefly at him! Her expression, friendly — and perhaps more — made him swivel forward again, awash in confusion. Was there some kind of double meaning in her words?

Paulina jumped in.

"Are you suggesting we may be as brainwashed as anybody else? But you said we're cynical!" She shook her head. "Unless ... unless *that's* the clue you were talking about."

"Could be," Mr. Castro said. "But first, what do you consider to be the principal propaganda message of our time? Come on, let's have it. Something really extensive and widespread, that we swim through every day."

Froggi spoke first. "Commercialism! Be a good consumer. Buy stuff!"

"Hmm, yes. By volume — in the sheer number of messages —

advertising can't be beat. But look at how thick-skinned the average person is toward commercials! I remember some old sci-fi novels predicted that people would march like morons to buy whatever they were told to. But reality is different. Every year advertisers struggle harder to amuse us, spending millions for a little name recognition. Nope. Try again."

"Religion," Dave said, succinctly, with his arms crossed and jaw set. That drew objections from Jamilla, Tasha and Jerome, who called Dave *intolerant.*

"The most paramount theme is conformity," suggested Arlene. "And reverence for the past. From an early age ... in China ...." Then she paused, suddenly unable to continue.

The teacher nodded. "It may surprise you to hear that I agree. Conformity is a potent theme that drives *every* society — at least every one I've heard of. Powerful forces push individuals to please their neighbors, and especially their tribal elites. At your age it's over-simplified with the term 'peer pressure.' Some of it comes from self-interest — it helps to have friends."

Ouch, Mark thought. He still felt confused by that look from Helene, a moment ago. Had there been some kind of under-meaning, for him alone?

"Especially back in olden times," Paulina said, with a furrowed frown. "Back in the caves, it must've been life-or-death to have friends. Maybe that's why it's built into us to worry so much about popularity."

"An interesting point," the teacher acknowledged. "Maybe you can find some references, pro and con, to share with us tomorrow." This time there were no groans. The topic hit most teens too close to home. Paulina bent over her tablet, tapping furiously.

"And yes," Mr. Castro continued. "Most societies actively preached conformity. Citizens were urged to resist disapproved influences and toe the line. This kind of indoctrination was common, in law and myth.

"But universal? Might our society be an exception?"

He paused.

"Can any of you name a recent movie that actively preached conformity? 'Be like everybody else and suppress your individuality'? How about any games, vids or popular novels? Can you come up with a single example? Even *one* in which the hero says everybody should be the same?"

This time, silence stretched for half a minute.

Slowly, as if it might be a mistake, Mark lifted his hand.

"I think the message in movies ... is nearly always the opposite."

"What do you mean?"

"Well, doesn't the hero, most of the time, kind of *stick it* to some evil rich guy? Or some nasty government agency?"

"Or powerful criminals, or some other conniving elite. Or else the mean supervisor, or the oppressive husband." Mr. Castro nodded. "Usually, it starts in the first ten minutes of a film. There has to be some clash with an authority figure in order for a modern audience to properly bond with the protagonist — the hero or heroine. Even if it's just a snide remark, mumbled about the boss or a neighborhood bigshot. If you really want the audience to hate the villain, show him oppressing someone. Or kicking an animal. Can anyone think of an exception?"

Mark could see his classmates wracking their brains. Especially Dave and Froggi, who clearly didn't like where this was heading.

"Suspicion of authority," the teacher said. "The theme fills our media tales, novels and videos. The main character has to display some quirk of individualism, some underdog eccentricity or independent streak, even if she starts out as an aristocrat or princess. Often it doesn't matter *which* authority figure gets defied. If the writer or director is politically right-of-center, it may be government or intellectuals. If she's more to the left, it could be a faceless, inhumane corporation or a smug aristocrat. Or vicious drug lords, or some foreign power ... or maybe a threat from outer space."

He turned around and wrote on the e-board. "One of your assignments will be to get examples. Tally how many modern movies you can find that preach suspicion of authority, and its companion message — *tolerance of eccentricity.*

"For comparison, also list films or videos, *if any,* that push the opposite message — conformity and/or intolerance of differences."

"But —" Dave McCarty sputtered. "How could suspicion of authority be propaganda! Are you suggesting that some conspiracy of secret masters one day decided — 'Hey, let's start a campaign so people will hate conspiracies and secret masters?' That doesn't even make sense!"

"Calm down, Dave. And no, I'm not saying it was planned ... though that might be an idea worth chewing on." He smiled. "I figure a more likely explanation is that we've been doing it ourselves, subconsciously, by paying to see entertainments that reinforce some- thing we —"

"— already believe," Kristin Gomez blurted, then rushed on to object. "But then why hasn't anybody noticed!"

"*I* noticed." Arlene Hsu raised her hand again. Some of the old shyness returned to her voice. "We *all* noticed, back in Guangdong. American movie heroes ... never show respect."

From behind him, Mark heard Helene Shockley respond. "I think maybe *we* don't notice because it's hard to —"

"— notice propaganda that you already agree with," Mark found himself finishing for her. He glanced at Helene apologetically, then away again quickly. There had been another friendly, enigmatic smile.

Now Dave was really angry. "You're saying we're *taught* to be indi- vidualists? That society *wants* us to defy authority? That —"

"That *you* didn't invent it, Dave?" murmured Paulina. "Any more than you invented the black leather look." She pointed at his studded jacket. "Yeah, I can live with that."

Not if looks could kill, Mark thought, as McCarty glared at her. A strangled noise gurgled, but before Dave could gather words, the class period bell rang.

"Check my web bot for the full assignment!" Mr. Castro called to those rushing for the door. Half a dozen students gathered near his desk, continuing to argue till the last possible moment. It illustrated why Mark had invited the teacher to be a witness, that crazy

Thursday night (it felt like a lifetime ago). In Mr. Castro's Class, you almost felt like you were in college, instead of a big warehouse for teens.

Mark wasn't one of those lingering behind. He hurried outside and turned to wait as throngs of students pushed past him in the hall. When Helene emerged, would there be something in her eyes again? If so, should he speak? What could he say?

Here she comes, he thought —

— only to be shouldered aside as someone much taller forged past. It wasn't a violent or aggressive shove. The rangy boy even muttered a friendly, reflex apology. No big deal; you got used to being jostled in the halls. And yet ....

Scott Tepper grinned, taking Helene's elbow as she emerged. The senior whispered in her ear and she laughed, shaking the coiled black ringlets of her hair. As they turned to head off together, Helene did offer Mark another glancing smile — it was friendly.

But that's all. Friendly. He must have imagined anything else.

He felt like a robot through Pre-Calc and English. In Chemistry, Alexandra tried to snap him out of it by threatening to set fire to his sleeve with the bunsen burner. She and Barry Tang — it was the one class they all took together — had to take care of the rest of their joint experiment without Mark's inept assistance.

What finally broke his spell of self-pity, a while later, was a sudden news flash that rocked the lunch court, sending everyone diving for cells and palm-links, even as sirens began wailing in the distance, toward a low line of desert hills.

A *terror attack,* murmured the soft, mechanical voices of several hundred wrist-phones and pen-cells, across the quad. An assault against the Contact Center — at the air base, just outside of Twenty-Nine Palms.

6

POP QUIZ

D *ad is there.*

   Mark's first impulse was to hurry toward the sirens, as fast as he could manage by foot or bike or by flagging down a car... all possibilities he dismissed in about a second. All seemed equally hopeless.

What he needed right now? Facts, quick and reliable.

Moving across the quad to where an open gate faced Rimpau Avenue, he pulled from his backpack that pair of Tru Vu specs the Channel Ten guys gave – or lent – to him that night, a few weeks ago. It was the first set he ever had a chance to try. Mark had been slyly practicing at home, navigating the goggle-like spectacles in much the same way that you'd use a super phone or pen-cell, accessing several levels of the Internet through his personal account – with the biggest difference being how the world web *surrounded* him with clickable choices, all of them overlaid upon his view of the real world.

Slipping them on, Mark saw the streets of Twenty-Nine Palms California through layers of *augmented reality*. The Tru Vu specs detected whatever his eyes happened to glance at, and wrote stuff on the inside of the glasses, guessing what he might want to know and offering links to even more data. All the nearby buildings had extra

ID markings painted over them – from the Shell gas station to his right, past Drannen's Hardware, the Food King and Pizza Habitat to Marshall Motors ... all bore info-tags that ballooned outward with added details, the very instant that he looked directly at something.

Students and pedestrians passing by ... they were also labeled. Twin camera dots on the Tru Vu rims scanned every face in stereo and compared it to an online registry, providing *tags*. No one using this tech would ever again be at a loss remembering another person's name. With practice, you might also access a guy-or-gal's sosh-sites ... or tap into gossip posted by an ex-girlfriend or ex-boyfriend, scanning all of it while looking right at the real person.

This kind of tech had been promised for decades. Major Bamford used a *heads-up display* each time he flew, relying on the *HUD* to draw flight and weapons data on the inner surface of the plane's bubble canopy. Civilians were used to getting augmented reality on their cells and pens and watches, offering simple displays, like direction arrows, so you never got lost, even in a strange town.

But *these* full overlay specs were another matter. Early versions had left people nauseated or caused accidents, delaying adoption by a decade or more. Only now – in the last year or so — were rich kids in the big cities finally sporting the things, walking around immersed in a double-layered world ... with *real* reality still plainly visible, but overlain with rich textures of color and information.

Right now, Mark had no interest in name tags! Lacking any other input device, he spoke commands aloud, not caring if he drew looks.

"Erase all! Now give me news feed on whatever's happening at the Base!"

That wasn't very specific. But the specs ought to guess which "base" he meant, and that he wanted emergency-level info.

Abruptly, several info-boxes opened in the periphery of Mark's vision, leaving clear the area right in front of him, so he could walk. One box blared a headline:

FLASH! Ninety-eight seconds ago Faux Presse
caught an alert — the U.S. military enclave

hosting the Garubis Guest is under attack!
Stay tuned for further ...

Trying to stay focused, Mark stared at that box and muttered "delete!" grunting satisfaction when it went away. He glanced at another, which zoomed outward, responding to his eye-interest. It showed a cam-image from some news crew, covering the festive crowd at the edge of the base. Only things weren't festive at the moment! Mark winced at the much-louder siren wail, enhanced by terrified screams from tourists and gawkers near the main gate. Bikers, cultists, neo-hippies and just-plain-folks were scurrying in all directions. The breathless reporter babbled –

"... still no word about what's happening. I'll stay up here on top of my van as long as I can, though if that turns out to be a terrible mistake I hope my husband and kids will understand. If only I could get higher ..."

Mark deleted that one too. Anyway, the reporter had given him an idea. *Get higher.* In order to look past the low buildings of the desert town. He took a quick spin to look at one option —

The school bell tower. An architectural ornament paid for by Augusto Video Montes, one of the founders of Cirrocco Corporation. Already, the slender edifice looked crowded, with a dozen students squeezed in the small atrium up top, staring east toward some commotion. Mark might have headed to join them ... only then he spotted Principal Jeffers striding purposefully toward the tower, with clear intent.

"Everybody get inside!" shouted the school cop, Mr. Perez. And for once, the jovial, pot-bellied retiree didn't wear his usual, affable grin. "All students take shelter in the gymnasium or other assigned places!"

Teachers were also spreading out, shouting for their charges to take cover, according to procedures everyone had practiced in the last drill. But the high school was an 'open campus' and Mark had already departed through the main gate. He was on Rimpau now, and running toward his only other option. The only other possible way to "get higher."

Marshall Motors – the Chevy dealer here in Twenty-Nine Palms, just a few doors east of the Food King. They kept an *advertising balloon* overhead during daylight hours, made of pixelated cloth that blared unbeatable offers in both real-reality and VR. On several occasions Mark had watched the owner use a winch to deploy or retract the display and he even helped once, when a freak sandstorm threatened to rip it all away. He had a crazy idea. So crazy that it just might —

As he neared, Mark noticed – *somebody's already hauling the balloon in.*

He also checked the time. Almost *three* whole minutes since the alarm first wailed. During that huge interval, ten thousand things could happen. And fear wrenched a coil in his gut as he now heard, in the distance, something more ominous than mere sirens. A series of faint *crump* and *whoosh* sounds — of air defense missiles launching out of vertical racks. He recognized the noises from an exercise Dad once let him attend.

Zig-zagging across the Food King parking lot, he vaulted the low barrier next to Sun Valley Real Estate and landed amid the shiny new cars...

...to find Alex Behr already at the winch, carefully tending the cable as it reeled in.

I might've figured. Jeez, she's a great pal and really useful. But it can get tiresome, always being a step behind her.

A couple of the X-guys were there too. Not the world's greatest wits, but *quick* on the uptake. Probably, they had already been thinking about the Marshall Motors balloon, for some stunt. Mark had. Who wouldn't? It made such a tempting *do something with me* target.

"Sup, dawg," Ricardo Chavez offered Mark a quick nod of greeting. So did Conner Mills and Dave McCarty, though Dave looked sweaty in his leather jacket, and hadn't said much to Mark since that tense discussion in History class.

"Sup n' hella-hola, compad," Mark answered quickly, on automatic. Because with his main attention he had been counting seconds. And roughly thirty beats after the missiles launched, there arrived a series of very faint, distant echoes, rumbles of what might be thunder. Then more whooshing sounds as the anti-aircraft battery resumed firing.

What's happening! Who's attacking? Could it be aliens? But the sky appeared empty and all innocent-blue.

Sidling closer to the winch, he spoke to Alex.

"Hey."

"Hey-back. What took ya?"

"Sue me," he shrugged. "Barry?"

"Sent him a ping. He'll be along. In time to miss everything."

"Usual. Empanado!"

"Yep."

Mark glanced around. Normally, you'd expect the Marshall Motors employees to interfere, or at least ask questions. But none of the salesmen were in sight. Probably doing something sensible, like seeking shelter. The clock in Mark's Tru Vu specs said four and a half minutes. The balloon had almost reached the ground. Ricardo and Conner were adapting a climbing harness to snap onto the cable.

"Dibs first," Dave claimed.

"Bull!" Ricardo responded. "It's my harness. Alex has to run the winch..."

"Hey! My parents both work at the Contact Center," she reacted hotly. "I got a better claim than anybody!"

"Yeah, well *all* of my living parents are there too," Mark interjected, reminding everybody he was already half-orphaned. "Plus... there's another reason I should go."

"Yeah what?" demanded Dave... who then stopped his protest short as Mark removed the Tru Vu goggles and held them up, so all could see the twin cameras and hi fidelity inputs. It went without saying. If he went up, wearing these, it would be like having their own *news and camera crew* up there. "You can tune in. See what I see."

Dave clearly wanted to contest the point, but Alex made a curt hand gesture and grunted. "No time to argue. Suit up, Bam!"

Mark jumped into position and put the specs back on, tugging and tying the stretchy headband-laces so they wouldn't jostle off, while Dave and Ricardo fastened harness buckles. "Ready to belay," he said.

"Belay on!" Alex cried.

Was there *anger* in her voice? As she yanked the release...

... and Mark had a sudden sense of falling. In a weird direction — *up!* The winch whined in seeming tempo with the emergency sirens, going off all over town. And, before he was halfway to the top, Mark heard an even more ominous sound – a fast-pitched, snare-drum stutter to the east. And he knew what it was. The chatter of high-speed Gatling guns. Vulcan close-in air defense cannons. Something must have made it past the long range missiles.

If only there were some way to *see* what was going on. Then Mark realized. *Idiot! You had that ability all along!*

"Specs!" He shouted, hoping the Tru Vus would understand his command. "Give me an overhead, real time satellite view of activity at the Twenty-Nine Palms air base!"

The machine tried to obey. A view box opened in his left-hand field of view – binocular and three dimensional, it zoomed in toward the Mojave Desert, flowing past the familiar mountains and salt pans...

...onto a sharp-edged zone that was as black and as dark as night!

SECURITY BLACKOUT IN EFFECT

"Damn!" Mark knew there were other ways. Someone who was really with-it about the latest tech might do a sift-search and find some camera aimed this way from the nature trails on Mount San Sebastian, or one of the Chinese commercial sats that were always overhead. *Maybe Alex should've been the one to go up, after all.*

Again, the shoosh of missiles and this time Mark saw their rocket exhaust trails as they sped upward from the base, arced left... and right... and away, apparently toward enemies looming in all directions! All directions except the civilian town. As yet, Mark saw no threat. No attackers. He did hear detonations. Frustratingly impossible to see!

Finally, the fast ascent began to slow... as he reached enough altitude to look over the main buildings of downtown Twenty-Nine Palms. And beyond them, lower, more shabby structures dating back to the 20th Century, when this was just a sleepy little training base, instead of a national center for high-tech testing.

Could that be why Na-Bistaka crashed here, in the first place? Was he spying on Cirrocco and its activities?

Then, at last, there it was. The military hangars and windowless warehouses and mysterious Cirrocco experimental facilities. The control tower and long, long runways. The far cluster of inflated buildings...

... and a *brilliant flash of light* that burst forth to crash into Mark from that direction, briefly overwhelming the spectacles, stinging his eyes, just before the Tru Vus darkened automatically, leaving him in pitch darkness. Overwhelmed and stunned, his first thought was simple:

Am I blind, or is it just the specs?

He reached up and tore them off – relieved to find his vision now just a bit speckled – then the concussion wave hit.

Moroni in the Andes! What did they destroy?

Rocking and pitching, his makeshift observation perch heaved and Mark barely held onto his lunch. Concern for his father, for the alien guest, for his country, all roiled in his gut for a few seconds, as the worst of the pressure front passed.

Then, far below, Alexandra Behr let out a warning shriek. Mark wrenched around to look where she was pointing – and spied something coming toward him fast out of the *west*, almost straight along Rimpau boulevard. Something fierce and fiery – a *dragon-machine* was his quick impression — heading this way!

Amid all the misfiring neurons of his brain, he realized. It had to be one of the attackers. A *drone* of some kind, swooping low over the town, almost down at street level, in order to evade radar and sneak in from behind.

It was coming straight at him! Mark kept his eyes open, thinking: *well, if I knock it down with my body, won't that be a fair exchange?*

Dad had sworn to make that kind of trade, as a military man, if ever it had to be done.

Maybe they'll bury me as a marine ...

Suddenly, he wanted to fight! Somehow, with anything. But he had nothing, except ...

His backpack. Still slung over his shoulder, a familiar weight unobstructed by the climbing harness. With a quick, practiced shrug, he let it drop to one fist in a motion that swung once ... twice ... and hurled it! An arc that swept the pack skyward, toward the onrushing drone ...

... as the pack spilled open, dropping textbooks, class notes, agendas, pencils and a picture of Helene Shockley, clipped out of the local paper when she'd been a finalist for Miss Teen Mojave.

Did that storm of paper chaff seem like a threat, just for an instant? The robotic drone must have sensed it — or Mark and the balloon – and abruptly decided to veer upward in avoidance. He felt its hot wake blow past and the world seemed to shake more than ever. The winch started screaming again, as Alex slammed it into reverse.

A series of popping, shredding sounds told of the balloon's progressive demise, as it started to lose buoyancy fast. Mark knew he'd be lucky to escape a broken leg, or worse.

And yet, he kept the foe in sight. The drone, already over the eastern part of town, struggled to drop back low, to resume its ground-hugging course, sneaking under the view of base-guardians as it –

Too late, you bastard!

There was another low staccato of the Gatling Gun ... and Mark felt a moment's triumph as the attacker machine exploded in a fireball.

Then, the ground came rushing at him fast.

7

ANNOUNCEMENTS

"**S**ome folks feel desperate to stop a Message from going out," Major Bamford explained late that night, around 1 a.m., between gulps of reheated stew. "Seeing public opinion shift, they decided to act."

How could Dad be so calm after today's near disaster? Mark's gut still churned over what he had witnessed first hand, a few hours ago, before landing in a harsh tuck-n-roll between two Pleiades hybrids. While the X Crew gathered what they could of his scattered backpack, Alex helped Mark nurse a sprained ankle into the lounge at Marshall Motors, where a crowd watched televised coverage of the attack. Which by then – thank heavens – appeared to be over.

Soon, the military released scenes of violent havoc, the remnants after more than a hundred ground-hugging robot aircraft had tried to swoop in from several directions, equipped with stealth technology. All of which suggested powerful backers with lots of funding.

One drone, filled with high explosives, had managed to swerve past the defense guns to strike next to the Contact Facility, demolishing a hangar where hybrid aircraft were being tested with morsels of alien science. It was the flash he saw, while riding the balloon.

Dad works there.

That had been his sole thought while watching images of the smashed, burning facility. He could hear distant ambulance sirens through the open door while, on TV, their strobe lights diffracted through clots of roiling smoke onto charred bodies. For a while Mark feared the worst, for his father and for the guest from the stars.

Then word came. Na-bistaka had remained comfortable the whole time, under those inflated domes. And Major Bamford sent hurried instructions –

Safe. Have dinner without me. Do homework as usual!

Then, much later over post-midnight cocoa, the tired officer described today's attack as only a close eyewitness could — starting with the sudden wail of alarms, followed by a *crump* and *hiss* of departing anti-aircraft missiles, then the brittle hum of close-in defense lasers and rapid-stuttering Vulcan guns and finally — deafening explosions. Though the attackers failed in their main goal, Dad's squadron lost two colleagues in the struck hangar. Working deep inside one of the experimental jets, they had been unable to take cover in time.

Hours later, clearly furious over the fatalities, Dad also seemed strangely composed — almost serene.

It's how you're supposed to act in a crisis, Mark thought, wishing he were made of the same stuff.

"I can take comfort in one thing," his father said. "The bastards have already lost."

THAT WAS THE LATEST NEWS, announced even as Major Bamford drove home for a late supper. The assassination attempt only served to consolidate world opinion. Shortly afterward, the International Contact Conference on the island of Malta took its vote, achieving that most remarkable accomplishment — *consensus.*

Planet Earth's human civilization, acting in unison, would help a stranded castaway from the stars.

The Message would go forth.

And immediately. So no one else could view murder as a viable alternative.

Like it or not, for better or for worse, humanity was committed.

"So ... what do you think will happen now, Dad?"

Mark's father smiled. The corners of his eyes creased near streaks of gray.

"Who can say? I know just one thing for sure, son — the world you'll live in will be different from the one my generation knew. We better hope that we succeeded in raising you kids well — to have agile minds and resilient souls. 'Cause it's a sure thing you'll need both."

Staying up till the wee hours, they watched televised coverage as workers prepared to cast forth *The Message,* from an antenna that had been prepared a few hundred miles north, in an isolated valley near the Nevada border.

Then came the phone call.

In all honesty ... Mark had been half expecting it.

THIS TIME, Barry Tang had permission. So did Tom Spencer and Chloe Mendel, from the geeky group that first recovered Na-Bistaka from his desert crash site. All five were invited to come and observe. Rushing to meet in the pre-dawn glow, they climbed aboard an Osprey II tiltrotor aircraft — one of eight in a convoy protected by two squadrons of Marine fighter jets.

Mark had no idea which of the other Ospreys carried the Interstellar Guest. In fact, there was a grim satisfaction in knowing: *one of the functions we're serving is as decoys, in case someone else tries an attack.*

At one point, peering through a dusty window pane, Mark felt certain that he recognized Major Bamford as one F35 cruised easily past. And Mark wondered. *What are those 'modifications' that Dad spoke of? Are we really making strides in adapting alien technologies? It can't have been very much so far. Not yet, with the little dribbles that Na-Bistaka's given us.*

The trip took less than an hour. Few words were spoken. Not many could be heard over the engine noise. Indeed, all five students were tired; few had slept much in 24 hours.

So they sat, pensively feeling the weight of history being made, each of them wondering – as were eight billion other human beings – *is this the right thing we're doing?* All the way to a landing strip in Southern California's Owens Valley, under the shadow of several giant radio telescopes.

There, a new construction towered, a spiral-shaped funnel of gleaming white and gray ceramic – it looked like a gigantic soft-serve ice cream cone — with great cables leading to three of the huge, steerable radar dishes. They were already aimed. Pointing at a particular corner of the deep-blue sky.

Funny, I would've pictured this happening at night, when you can see which stars, which constellation ...

Alex helped Mark limp out of the aircraft, and handed over the cane he had borrowed for his sprain. Only when he thanked her, she turned away. Clearly, Alex was still miffed over the way he had used unfair – both logical and emotional – tactics to seize the balloon ascent for himself. And maybe Alex had a point. They might never know if his maneuver with the backpack had been helpful in destroying that sneaker-drone. Or (more likely) just a silly gesture. Who knows? Maybe she was miffed over that picture of Helene, floating down to fall onto the winch even as Alex struggled to control it and save Mark's life.

Well, well. There were levels of upset, and he knew this mood. She was already getting over it and would be fine, soon. So long as he was extra nice for a bit.

A massive bunker lay beneath that spiral tower. Mark never even glimpsed the alien till they were all inside, taking assigned places in a control room that seemed half NASA Mission Control and half the bridge out of some Star Trek movie. Then he spotted Na-Bistaka, a small figure in silken red, surrounded by dignitaries and senior technical people, like Alex's mom.

Nobody seemed much interested in ceremony. The decision had

been made. Time now to implement the world consensus. The alien handed the Chief Scientist a small block, like a sugar cube, containing a coded message, which she proceeded to drop into a slot ... and a countdown began as dials showed energy levels building.

"Yipe!" Barry Tang muttered to Alex. "Do those dials really measure in *gigajoules?*"

Alex whistled in awe, then glanced at Mark, who nodded in sage wonder, wearing his own look of amazed appreciation ... and making a mental note to find out, later, what a gigajoule was.

Only during the final countdown did the hooded, silken robe turn as Na-Bistaka scanned the human beings lined up along the tiers behind him. That narrow snout seemed to pause, briefly just once, as those large eyes spotted Mark and the other kids from Twenty-Nine Palms High School. That strange, double-elbowed arm lifted. A knobby, wandlike finger pointed, briefly.

And Mark Bamford tried *not* to think of his old nickname.

Then, it was time.

The moment that the pulse launched forth, Mark felt a sudden tightness in his throat. There were no other signs for the uninformed visitor – no spectacular special-effects sounds or flashes. Nor sparking, overloaded circuit boards. Did the abrupt crawling sensation along his spine come from some side effect of *quantum tunneling* when the signal burst forth?

Did everyone on Earth feel the same thing, at the very same instant?

Or was it a psychological thing — a symptom of realizing at last...

That's it. No turning back.

One thing he sure didn't expect ... and he doubted that anyone else did either.

He never imagined the Garubis would reply so soon.

8

HONORED GUESTS

A rescue ship arrived just ten days after the Message was sent.

It entered orbit four thousand kilometers up — a giant cylinder that rolled swiftly around its long axis. Mirrorlike, it reflected the glitter of starlight, and vastly dwarfed the International Space Station, orbiting far below.

"In that orbit," one scientist commented, "they're just cruising through the Van Allen radiation belts. Either they and their equipment are far less prone to radiation damage ... or else they have really great shielding. Either way, they're showing off."

"Yes, well, either way," added another NASA official, stating the obvious, "it makes sure we won't be coming up there to knock on their door. They'll be coming to us."

Communications from the star-galleon were brusque at first, consisting of a simple statement in the Garubis tongue, demanding to speak with Na-bistaka. When that connection was made, linking directly to the alien's habitat near Twenty-Nine Palms, a whirl of chuttering conversation ensued, so rapid that it taxed the new translation programs. However, one exchange came through perfectly clear.

How did the natives treat you?

The world waited tensely, then sighed in relief at Na-bistaka's reply.

After some initial discomfort ... better than expected.

What followed seemed harder to decipher. One expert thought there was a tone of disappointment in the starship's reply. Something that might be translated as — *too bad.* Other linguists dismissed this guess as pure imagination, and illogical to boot. After all, how could such a reaction even make sense?

Anyway, public attention soon shifted to a brief spat between the U.S. State Department and the U.N. Contact Commission, bickering over where to invite the Garubis to land. They finally agreed that, even though the Americans had proved worthy of continuing their leading role, Washington D.C. was too much of a national symbol. And the California desert was too isolated.

When the visitors affirmed that they could touch down a lander with high accuracy and only slight disruption, a bold but popular decision was reached. For the reception to take place near United Nation headquarters, right inside the world's densely-packed "down-town." During some terse back-and-forth, the ship-master curtly insisted on one perfect site.

In forty-eight hours the Garubis would bring their rescue vehicle to Memorial Park, on lower Manhattan Island, in the City of New York.

IT HAPPENED ON A SATURDAY, so they made a party of the event in the Bamford living room. Dad worked at the kitchen table, poring over recent photos of the orbiting spacecraft, while Mark and his friends scarfed popcorn and soda in front of a media array featuring several borrowed screen-sets made of pixelated cloth and assorted holo-links.

Twenty-Nine Palms seemed a ghost town. Pizza delivery places were the only businesses at work, and they had a three-hour backlog.

Even the swarm of TV vans that had staked out the nearby air base for months finally dispersed that morning, when Na-bistaka's plane departed under escort by a squadron of Marine Corps fighter jets. For a while, reporters prowled the desert community like hungry wolves, stopping occasionally by the Bamford house in hope of a bite. Mark never emerged. Alex and Barry had avoided the reporters by the simple expedient of parking their bikes in the next street and then vaulting over the Fortinis' back fence. (Well, Alex vaulted. Barry grunted and slithered.)

Anyway, it seemed logical to meet here. Alex's parents were out of town, having gone ahead to help prepare the way for Na-bistaka in New York. And the Tang family, for some reason that Mark never fathomed, did not own a pixelvee, or even an old fashioned TV.

So they settled in to watch as humanity's important moment unfolded.

But not right away. At first, all the webs and cables and satellite dishes conveyed was wave after wave of *talk*. Conjecture and groundless speculation. What kind of law reigned out there on the vast starlanes? Was there a Galactic Federation of some sort? Na-bistaka had affirmed that the Garubis weren't alone out there. He even mentioned a few species names and sketched a few strange faces ... then stopped providing any further information, saying that such things weren't in his area of expertise.

We never did find out what his job really is, Mark pondered. *Or why he came all this way to Earth.* The xeno-visitor was very good at keeping things close to the chest.

"Well, after all," one pundit ventured. "If *you* were accidentally thrown into a first contact situation, wouldn't you find it wise to keep quiet, till specialists could be called in? To do otherwise might be irresponsible!" The expert blabbed on that way for quite some time, apparently unaware of any irony.

While professional talkers kept the waiting world distracted, New York prepared, once again, to take center stage as World Party Headquarters. Bridges and tunnels groaned as crowds of the timid left town ...

... and replacement throngs poured in, eager to help celebrate the dawn of a new era. Clearly, it was a matter of temperament, and humanity had all kinds. "Diversity is strength," commented one of the onscreen pundits. But Mark recalled something else that his biology teacher had said, a year ago.

Diversity is the grist of evolution.

BERTHED at the waterfront next to Memorial Park, two giant cruise liners were being frantically readied to host visiting star-emissaries, in case they wanted more room than a mere landing craft could provide. Ocean liners seemed ideal because they were already relatively self-contained, almost like a spaceship, down to storing waste products aboard sealed tanks. Even the atmosphere could be altered to some extent, through sealed air conditioning systems. Anything the visitors found distasteful could be removed and whatever they liked could be swiftly brought aboard. Helicopters and barges were already rushing in every kind of food that Na-bistaka had found pleasant during his stay.

Meanwhile, on Manhattan's East Side a short distance uptown, the U. N. dropped all other business as presidents, royalty and other dignitaries arrived to take part in the most important meeting ever.

Nor were 'just people' to be left out. Along vacated First Avenue, a series of giant canopies served the world's raucous special interest groups — from environmental and religious associations to industrial and labor organizations. From scientific academies to bickering ethnicities. Huge banners spread open, offering greetings in many tongues, or else appealing for miraculous intervention. Anyone with a special problem seemed to be there, and the Big Apple stretched to accommodate them all.

Instead of panic – people who felt that way had already left town – the mood seemed to say, *this belongs to everyone.* Welcoming honored guests. Keeping them safe. Handling a million sober details and preparing for ten times as many contingencies. Listening to all concerns ... while giving free rein to celebration. Sure, it was impossible. But this city could manage it.

Besides, who knew yet which of humanity's nagging troubles might be solved by Contact? Some enthusiasts were bound to be disappointed while others might have their wildest dreams come true. Immortality? Warp drive? Teleportation? Realistic 'holodecks' that offered experience better than real life?

Wiser heads cautioned: some problems might have no easy answer. Others could fall into the disappointing category of 'later, when you're ready.'

"They may be almost as confused by us as we are by them," mused one sage. "We can't assume, for example, that they'll give us a magic formula for world peace. We've been slowly learning *how* to do that all by ourselves, for several generations, with actual per capita rates of violence falling steeply ever since the Second World War. What we lacked, in finishing the job, has been the will."

Others disagreed.

"Imagine asking the Garubis to serve as neutral *arbitrators,*" a competing commentator gushed. "They'd have nothing to gain by one side winning unfairly over another. We could settle so many ancient disputes — Palestine, Kashmir, Korea, Carolina, the Congo!"

The ensuing argument grew so heated that Mark changed channels.

Scientists appeared to care more about what could be learned about nature's laws.

"Of course, I have mixed feelings," said one Nobel Prize winner. "I spent my whole life becoming a top expert in my field. Here on Earth and — so far as we once knew — in the whole universe."

He laughed. "Now I must go back to school. Elementary school, perhaps!"

Mark noted that the graying researcher didn't look all that chagrined by the prospect of losing his 'expert' status, or even returning to basics. In fact, it seemed to delight him. *Some people are just wiser and more flexible than I'll ever be,* he thought with a sigh.

On one thing every commentator seemed to agree.

"We'd know by now, if the Garubis were outright hostile," one of them summed-up. "I doubt we'd have been able to fight off a humungous ship like that. So, at worst, the universe is about to open up to humanity. Maybe a lot."

One historian then arched her eyebrow, adding — "We may soon have new tools, helping us become a whole lot richer, while at the same time making us *feel* much poorer, in comparison to others out there. Keeping some perspective may be crucial. Let's learn from the mistakes made by *both* sides during past episodes of first contact — between Earthling cultures a few centuries ago. We must be bold and dynamic, while at the same time keeping our feet firmly planted in reality. On Mother Earth."

AROUND TWO IN THE AFTERNOON, even as Na-bistaka's plane arrived at Newark Airport, amateur astronomers reported visually sighting the Lander. A *disk* had peeled off one end of the great, orbiting cylinder and was now dropping through Earth's atmosphere like a frisbee, spinning as it threw off gouts of friction heat.

"Dang, it's big!" Barry said as reports poured in from along the vessel's glide path. "Maybe five city blocks."

Mark glanced at the cleared area in Memorial Park, wedged between the two great waterfall fountains where mighty towers used to stand. National Guard troops surrounded the specified landing site, facing outward to keep back the crowds.

Some trees may not survive, he guessed, though still there should be enough room. On TV, several pundits fretted about the lander avoiding all the tall buildings nearby, a sensitive issue in that particular spot.

After making sure his friends had all they needed, Mark went to check on Dad, who still sat at the kitchen table, poring over photographs and charts. Officially, nothing was supposed to be top secret about this interstellar contact. Still, it surprised Mark that his father had brought this material home for the weekend.

On one side were pictures taken by orbital satellites of the gleaming Garubis star galleon. To the right were images of a much smaller craft — the lifeboat that brought Na-bistaka down to the Southern California desert for his initial encounter with "human larval forms" in their strange, high school tribes.

Major Bamford tapped a photo taken after the escape capsule had been unburied by an Air Force recovery team. "This still puzzles me," he told Mark.

"What does?"

Dad shook his head.

"What doesn't? We never learned what 'malfunction' forced Na-bistaka to make an emergency landing ... or indeed, what happened to his ship. Was it completely destroyed? Is it stranded on the far side of the moon?"

"Maybe we'll find out when his people go salvage it," Mark suggested. Then he added with a grin. "I bet *you* hope it's abandoned. Left behind as scrap. Then you might get sent to look it over?"

They had discussed this, of course. Dad was no astronaut, but soon there might be so much to do in space — so many urgent jobs — that even a regular old jet jockey (with high-tech intelligence background) could get the nod! Mark hoped so, for his father's sake.

"That could be. Only —"

"Only what, Dad?"

The major chewed his lip briefly.

"Only I keep wondering about these streaks right here ... along the side of the lifeboat. That hull is incredibly tough, yet some terrific heat seems to have scorched it."

"Heat ... from entering the atmosphere?"

"I don't think so. I have a hunch that it came from some kind of weapons fire."

Mark blinked a few times.

"But ... that would mean —"

"Hey you two Bamfords!" Alex called from the living room. "Get in here and watch this! They're about to land!"

Dad stood up and gave Mark's shoulder a squeeze as he walked past, ready to leave the photos and just play spectator for a while, as history was made onscreen. But Mark hesitated, lingering to stare down at one picture showing tracks of burnt and melted ceramic — streaks of damage along a gleaming shell.

COLUMBUS IS ROWING ASHORE *and natives are partying on the beach,* he thought, watching festive throngs gather in New York.

Not everybody was unworried. Would the big descent craft arrest its plummet atop a roaring column of rocket flames, belying their assurance of a *gentle landing?* Standards could differ, after all. Setting a whole city ablaze might be their idea of 'minor damage'.

Or would they intimidate aboriginal Earthlings by hovering overhead, dauntingly silent, as portrayed in countless sci-fi films?

Antigravity is impossible, Na-bistaka had maintained, dismissing the very notion as another useless 'larval fantasy.'

Well, okay then. Mark pondered. Let's see what you have instead.

"We've got visual sighting," said one announcer. Cameras began showing a glowing disk whose color changed as it cooled, from bright blue, hard to make out against the sky, down to a fiercely harsh green, then iridescent yellow-red. As descent brought it closer, commentators pointed out that the configuration only remotely resembled legendary 'flying saucers' that people claimed to have seen over generations. There were no cupolas or bulges or flashing lights, for instance. There was no tapered edge. Nor did it dart about. Progress was swift but also ponderously natural.

Above New Jersey, the space vessel dropped below the speed of sound, flying no more than a thousand feet or so overhead. Local citizens under the path reported sudden blasts of hot air, followed by manic cyclones or dust-devils. Leaves and tree-branches whirled in its wake.

"So, it stays up by thrusting air downward," Major Bamford deduced with a nod. "Just as we thought. No magical suspensor beams or gravity pulsors. They use Newton's Laws, as we do — though the *energy source* for such a system ..."

Mark saw a gleam of ambition in his father's eye. He wanted a close look at whatever powered that ship.

The Garubis vessel slowed down to a relative crawl over the Hudson, surrounded by federal helicopters that kept swarms of news-choppers and private drones at bay. Below, the river's surface bucked and spumed, creating a low, artificial fog.

When that thing touches down, it'll do more than just smudge the Heroes Memorial, Mark thought. On the other hand, slabs of marble can be replaced.

Then, still several hundred meters short of Manhattan, the ship halted — hovering on a column of hot, pressurized air. A large panel slid aside, revealing an opening along one flank.

Suddenly, a stream of objects spewed out, hundreds of them, perhaps thousands, all streaking toward New York!

"My God," said Barry. "Are those *missiles?* Could they be attacking?"

"Don't be silly," responded Alex, though her voice quavered. "There must be another explanation."

Mark winced as the horde of cylindrical-shaped objects swooped down toward the cameras and crowds near the park, raising shrieks of alarm. For several seconds he didn't breathe ...

... until abrupt order emerged out of the decelerating tubes — each of them now visibly hollow inside. Several dozen of the cylinders plummeted to the park's hard loam between sets of trees, sinking deep. Others followed, clamping onto the tops of those that came before, as they were topped in turn, stacking upon each other, one at a time.

Rapidly, three *spires* began to form — equidistant from each other and surrounding one of the Memorial's famous, square, inverted fountains. Before their eyes, the trio of columns stacked higher and higher, rising with uncanny speed.

"It's a self-assembling platform!" Barry announced, crouching to get a better look. "With one of the big waterfall pools right in the middle!"

It took less than a minute for the cloud of darting cylinders to visibly shrink, as scores and then hundreds of automatic drones mated together, piling higher, aggregating themselves neatly into three steeples that leaned slightly inward, toward each other. The crowd below changed its tone just as rapidly, shifting from fear to awe, and then delight, watching three delicate minarets climb higher and higher, soon topping the nearest of Manhattan's skyscrapers.

Now the great disk of the landing craft started moving in, leaving behind the fog it had kicked up from the Hudson's waters. The spindly platform was ready, a towering *tripod* several hundred meters high, casting long afternoon shadows all the way past Wall Street to the East River. By the time the Lander fully settled in place, shutting down its roaring engines, Mark realized — the Garubis had not lied. They said they would come down in a densely populated Earth-city without causing any damage.

Except to our egos, he thought.

Who needs anti-gravity when you can do stuff like that?

THE VISITORS MADE IT CLEAR — things were to be done in a specific order.

First, repatriate Na-bistaka. Then talk.

That seemed a little churlish, by human standards. It might have been more reassuring to share greetings and pleasantries along the way. Have a little ceremony. Exchange some gifts. Offer them keys to the city.

("No!" one expert objected. "They might take the 'key' symbolism literally!")

The Jersey subway tunnel had been closed all day, in order to bring the xeno guest-castaway from the airport by a safe route — one terminating in a secure zone just beneath the titanic landing tower. Much of the world's population watched as Na-bistaka, in his enveloping scarlet gown, rode a train underneath the Hudson with a dozen escorting dignitaries from the highest levels of human society. Then escalators carried the group upward through the vacant commuter station, all the way to the surface plaza — whereupon his appearance triggered noisy cheers from the surrounding throng, and thousands more peering from buildings on all sides.

I can see why they chose this site, Mark pondered. *Quick access from the river, so their jet blast didn't hit any major buildings. Perfect security access by underground rail. And this perch, above one of the big memorial pools, will let water absorb more heat when they take off. Sure, some trees got squished and there'll be repairs, but nothing huge.*

Still, looking at the two square, inverse fountains, he pictured the great towers that once stood there... and couldn't help wishing the star-guests had chosen someplace else. There on the expansive tiled piazza, the Heroes Memorial – and even the nearby Freedom Tower skyscraper — seemed dwarfed underneath the towering Garubis tripod. Spindly legs flexed as individual tubes adjusted to the tug and push of wind. (Technical experts calculated, breathlessly, that each of the hollow pillars might weigh less than a city bus!)

The overall effect was to make the quivering tripod look alive, as if ready to advance on legs over a thousand feet high.

"The Martians in H.G. Wells used tall tripods, to stomp about and crush humanity's mightiest works —" commented Barry, and he seemed about to add more, but Alex hushed him.

Na-bistaka and Earth's accompanying emissaries now approached one of these towering limbs. The crowd murmured as an opening appeared, a *door* in the bottommost cylinder at the plaza level, revealing a dimly-lit elevator car.

Nobody emerged. No one could be glimpsed inside.

Quickening his stride with apparent eagerness, Na-bistaka moved ahead of his human escorts, who followed nervously. Without pausing, the scarlet-clad alien then entered the waiting lift without a word.

He did not even turn around as the doors closed behind him, leaving the Mayor of New York, the Vice-President of the United

States, the Secretary General of the United Nations, and Imam Suleiman — representative of the Ecumenical Council of Faiths — all just standing there.

For several stunned minutes, none of them moved. Nobody seemed willing to be first. But as twilight began to fall, the disappointed luminaries turned, one by one, and began drifting away — robbed of their former dignity.

"Well," summed up Alexandra Behr, tossing up a piece of popcorn to catch in her mouth. "*That* was rude."

As the initial shock wore off, some TV commentators tried to make excuses for the Garubis, repeating the aphorism — *Do not judge others by your own values. Their ways may be different. We must allow for aliens having unique and possibly strange notions of courtesy.*

That refrain continued for a while, on every broadcast and cable channel ... till one person finally dared to speak up with a dissenting point of view. It was the woman college professor Mark had seen earlier, who had urged that humanity stay both bold and well-grounded.

"Hogwash!" she muttered now.

"Clearly and logically, it's up to any visitor to learn and adjust to native customs, and *we're* the natives, here! They're supposed to be the smart, sophisticated ones, right? Experienced at contact? Yet *we* took care of all the language translation difficulties. We took pains to learn the Xeno's needs. We transmitted the Message, rolled out the red carpet and offered every hospitality ..."

She had to stop, half-choked with anger, taking a moment before resuming.

"They're guests in our home, and one *should* accommodate guests — even bend over backwards. But we've done all that, and more!

"Let's not bend over so far now that we can't see the obvious, right in front of our faces.

"Friends and fellow Earthlings ... I'm afraid our *guests* have just peed on our carpet."

≈

NO ONE WAS ESPECIALLY SURPRISED, then, to hear the engines of the landing craft start to warm up. National Guardsmen pushed and the crowd backed away as hot wind blasted down from the tripod, kicking up a fog from the fountain directly below and sending billows of dust whipping down the handmade canyons of Manhattan.

"We should have insisted on a trade," Barry Tang said. "Demanded rent. A rescue fee! Kept ahold of the little jerk till they paid some of that old *quid pro quo.*"

"I guess so," Mark sighed. It was obvious now, in retrospect.

And yet, generosity had felt so *right*. To offer hospitality and kindness without any overt sign of greed. For a month or so, the whole world had seemed astonished and rather pleased with its own new, altruistic attitude. Defying all the cynics who routinely despised human nature, most people took the high road out of a sense of ...

Well, maybe it was pride.

We may be poor natives. But we have honor. Honor that we either ignored or horribly abused among ourselves, for all of recorded time. Still, it existed. All cultures shared the core notions.

Underneath everything, when we decide to pay attention, that honor may be stronger than we ever suspected.

Only now, was that turning out to be a mistake, after all?

The disk lifted from its perch atop the towering tripod, and at once the three-legged platform started dissolving, from the top down, into countless small, hollow drones that swirled to join a spinning cloud. Like a genie re-entering its lamp, the swarm drew inward, converging and funneling to the belly of the hovering craft. When every last one had been recovered, the vessel turned over the Hudson, then southeast to cruise over the Statue of Liberty, blasting the giant sculpture with hot effluent as it climbed and accelerated over the Atlantic.

People in Manhattan — and on all continents — watched in sour disappointment. There would be no speeches today. No welcoming ceremonies. No negotiations.

No party.

Then came a final surprise.

Even as the lander passed out of sight, a chuttering sound abruptly surged from every radio and television set, evidently broadcast by the giant Garubis star galleon, high overhead. Caught by surprise, most networks needed a few moments to seek help with translation. A group of amateur linguists from Manila beat all the universities and government agencies by several seconds, providing a first English-language version of the aliens' announcement.

We acknowledge that you have done us a service.
We acknowledge that we are in your debt.

The pause that followed might have been deliberate. Or simply punctuation. For emphasis.

Only, then came the kicker.

We hate being indebted to vermin.

Mark's jaw dropped. Nor was he alone. There had to be something wrong with the translation! Perhaps it was somebody's idea of a joke.

Only then alternate versions began appearing on different channels — from the U.S. government, the Beijing Institute for Advanced Science, and from academics who had worked directly with Nabistaka. All paraphrasings of the Garubis broadcast converged on the same general meaning.

We shall discharge this debt as soon as possible.

We shall repay you with something of high value
from a List of Traditional Restitutions
For The Young and Hungry.

We shall do this before your planet spins another six times.

Then, in gladness, we will depart.

Trying to expunge
memory of your noxious odors.

For the longest time, not a single pundit or commentator spoke. The airwaves of Planet Earth were more quiet than they had been in generations. Perhaps since the days of Marconi.

Oh, this wasn't the very *worst* possible kind of alien contact. But, almost without any doubt, it was the most insulting.

Of course, not everybody saw things the same way. Barry Tang finally broke the silence in the Bamford home with a chortle of eagerness.

"Cool!" he said, rubbing his hands avariciously.

"I wonder what they're gonna give us."

9

STUDY HALL

Much to Mark's surprise, life went on during the week that followed.

At Twenty-Nine Palms High School, preparations went into high gear for both Prom Night and the Desert Carnival. Nearly all of the posters depicting merry gray aliens were defaced by vandals, so Principal Jeffers declared a change in theme. Some leftover decorations from last year's "Underwater Charm" dance were hastily gussied up — by the small minority of students who cared about such things.

As the big day approached, workers finished constructing a compact amusement park at one end of the athletic field, including a couple of high-intensity Hurl Rides. More carnival people arrived in a small caravan to finish preparations, with a coin-pitch booth (for fundraising) and even an animal act, with some trained dogs and a performing chimp. The same carnies — tattooed and surly, but generally harmless — had been doing the Desert Carnival at TNPHS for years.

With midterms over, seniors started gathering in clusters on the school steps, signing yearbooks and vowing to keep in touch after dispersing to various colleges, or else employed independence.

Meanwhile, Mark's fellow juniors felt the approach of their own turn at the top of the school totem pole. Some began firing up campaigns for office in the coming school elections.

Still, any resemblance to normality was superficial. Teens who never used to pay attention to current events — even those who couldn't name a senator or governor – now rolled up their sleeves and checked their forearm web-tattoos between class, in case some news had come down from the orbiting starship.

Everyone knew that Friday would be the big day. One that might change the world. It roused a lot of contradictory feelings.

While bagging groceries at Food King, Mark felt keenly aware of how many people eyed him — not just kids from TNPHS, but towns-people in general. Some offered sour looks, as if the rudeness shown by Na-bistaka's folk had somehow been his fault. Others scanned the tabloid magazines that lined his checkout counter. Every issue blared speculations about what *The Gift* would turn out to be. Conjectures ranged from cancer cures to smart pills, from the secret of life to a new weight-loss diet that really works. Sometimes, people reading these headlines would smile at Mark, or pat him on the back as they departed. Others left oversized tips at his bagging station.

The first time that happened, Mark put every nickel into the collection bin for Muscular Dystrophy. After that, he gave all the accumulated tips to a homeless lady he often saw on the corner, roaming with her possessions piled in a shopping cart. Her reaction, to mutter and look away, suited him fine.

One thing Mark knew – with a rising sense of gloom — if the aliens' *Gift* turned out to be a disappointment, he was going to have to leave the town of Twenty-Nine Palms. Maybe California. Heck, was there any place on Earth where he could hide, if humanity didn't like the Garubis' notion of 'repayment'?

A gift appropriate for *vermin*. Yeah, that boded well. Right.

Maybe it was already time to start packing.

"What would *you* ask for?" Mr. Castro demanded, during history class, right after that fizzled 'first contact' was broadcast live from New

York on a fateful Saturday night. The assignment: think up your own best guess about the Gift and come prepared to defend your choice on Wednesday — just two days before the world would find out the truth.

First though, Mark was a member of an athletic team. He owed it to the others to at least show up, to do his best.

STILL, it was kind of hard to concentrate at the climbing wall.

True, the girl soccer players had vanished. Even the football team was on hiatus with their playing field given over to the Carnival — and no jocks were using weights below. It seemed a good time for the X Crew to get some practice in.

Only this time there was so much noise and bustle nearby, as big roustabouts shouted, hammering pegs into the ground, setting up tents and amusement rides. In recent years, the little fair had grown much bigger than a High School homecoming dance, drawing in pretty much the whole valley on the second night. And now the carnies were adding even more, betting that the brief notoriety of Twenty-Nine Palms might draw in tourists from the coast.

I hope not, Mark thought, perhaps a bit disloyally. It was the school's biggest fundraiser—and this year, the climbing wall would be a part of it, raising money for X Crew shirts and sweats. Even so, he didn't hanker to see the outside world return, with its glaring scrutiny.

Speaking of scrutiny. One of the carnies, wandering by on break, had stationed himself nearby, chain smoking. A big fellow, with dusky complexion and a black bristly beard, he leaned against a wall, as if helping to keep it from collapsing. His bare arms bore inked designs of snakes and eagles. Mark wished he'd go away.

"Come on, Bamford! You're on the clock!"

This time it was Ricardo Chavez egging him on, from just over-head. *All right.* Mark concentrated. *Stick to the rhythm.*

Left foot goes to the Doorknob ... set it ... now shift weight ... right heel

*onto Bignose ... and PUSH as left hand shoots for the Wedgie ... jam it good
...*

He had given nicknames to every hand and foothold in the memorized route. Not very realistic, of course. In life, authentic challenge always comes from variety and surprise, especially in real rock climbing, with no ascent ever the same twice. But this route was part of the standardized prelims. A pure speed race. Moving systematically and by rote, he quickly made it to the top with only a minimum of sweat.

Ricardo released Mark's clip and Barry Tang, who had attached himself to the crew as equipment manager, quickly coiled the rope. "Not bad," Ricardo said, looking at his stopwatch. He showed the time to the Hammar twins.

Nick Hammar was indifferent, offering a shrug as he flirted with Alex, helping her out of her harness, Alex slapped his hand at one point, but laughed, seeming anything but angry.

"I guess you won't shame us," Nick's brother Greg commented.

Mark glanced at the time. *Shame us? Only Alex is quicker. And she's half spider. We'll do fine at the first match ... if that sort of thing matters anymore.*

Churning at the back of his mind was the same thing distracting nearly everybody else — how the Garubis "gift" might change everything.

Already there were voices, in the media and among leading thinkers, who seriously proposed that humanity should *refuse* the gratuity. And not just out of pride or xenophobia. After all, how could people trust a benefaction given by aliens who call your kind "vermin"? No matter how attractive the dingus turned out to be, you had to worry and wonder. Could it wind up being like the bait in a mousetrap? Or the honeyed ingredient in roach poison? Even some of those who had been most enthusiastic were now suggesting that the Gift be extensively tested ... perhaps on an isolated island, or even the Moon ... before exposing humanity and Earth as a whole.

Alex said that her parents were still in a state of shock. After all of their hard work, taking care of Na-Bistaka, clearly they had allowed their hopes to climb, like kids before a birthday. Expectations of something like gratitude. Or at least a pat on the head.

If the others were pensive, Ricardo seemed unflappable, true to the spirit of X. "Come on," he said, after they were finished cleaning up and the Hammar boys hurried off to meet their ride.

"Bring your gear. I got a surprise for you guys."

Our gear? Mark shouldered a rope and his bag of climbing tools, glancing at Alex, who shrugged, as much in the dark as he was. Her tank top exposed shoulders that were a tad more ripped — more muscular — than Mark generally found attractive in a girl. Still, on Alex it seemed right enough.

Perhaps sensing his scrutiny, she threw on a sweatshirt and stepped after 'Cardo, letting Mark and Barry take up the rear. Soon they were approaching the main building of Twenty-Nine Palms High, apparently empty as a ghost town, an hour after the student throng made its daily escape.

"I've checked carefully," the X Boy said, stopping next to the Bell Tower — a decorative feature that jutted from one end of the two story structure, giving it a faux, California Mission feel. There had never been a bell.

"This is a total blind spot. Nobody can see us here, except from the direction we just came."

Mark looked around. It seemed plausible. "So?"

Ricardo dumped his gear and started chalking his hands.

"So? I'm going up. Anyone else coming?"

Mark stared at the boy, and then at the planned route. There were very few holds or protrusions. "Has anybody done it before?"

"Doubt it. The tower's only a couple years old and I figure we would of heard. 'Til a few weeks ago, there was an easy climb up the inside spiral steps, but ever since the attack, Principal Jeffers had it double padlocked."

"Hm ... so?"

"So I'm gonna carve my initials where nobody but another climber can see." Ricardo whipped out a chisel that was almost certainly against the school's zero-tolerance rules. "Relax, I didn't smuggle a weapon on campus. I borrowed this from wood shop."

Mark wasn't sure the principal would accept that distinction. But Alex stepped up.

"I'm in," she said.

Really? Mark blinked at her. Then Barry Tang eagerly spoke.

"I'll go topside and belay," he said, tucking a rope inside his bulky jacket. When the others stared, he said: "What? You're the only people with skills? I cracked that new lock of Jeffers within two days after he installed it. Been up the spiral and into the bell tower several times since. I'll head up now and fix a safety rope."

"Well... okay but don't get seen!" Ricardo called after, as Barry hurried off, disappearing around a corner. The X boy secured his chalk bag and straightened his knit cap before stepping inside a narrow space — barely a decorative niche — between the jutting tower and the building proper.

"Chimney ascent," Mark commented, feeling a rising sense of appreciation ... against his better judgment. "It's been a long time."

Alex nodded. "It does seem kinda dumb to call ourselves a *climbing team* when all we've done is a wimpy, artificial knob-wall. I was gonna take you all out to some nice pipes and crevices in Joshua Tree, over break. But this is cool, too."

Well, well, Mark thought, pondering her tone. *Look at Miss Nonconformist.* Alex was normally kind of proper. But maybe she felt this was her moment to prove something. "Wing stretching" as Dad called it. Teen rebellion didn't always make sense. Sometimes, it wasn't even clear what you were trying to prove.

Okay, he thought, peering up at the route that 'Cardo proposed. *What's the worst that can happen?*

Mark instantly regretted posing it that way. He rephrased the question in his mind. *How much trouble can we get into?*

Like all climbers, from amateur to pro, he knew about legendary "urban ascents," when dashing daredevils challenged skyscrapers like the Chicago Sears Tower, transfixing newscams and millions of viewers around the world. Security experts kept erecting barriers to prevent such stunts, and those who succeeded were sure to be arrested upon reaching the top. Still, there seemed to be an unwritten set of conventions about what kind of punishment you could expect. If no one else was endangered, if no property got harmed, and assuming no greedy or nasty motives were involved, it often came down to a couple of nights in jail, a modest fine, and some weeks assigned to community service. In several famous cases, that meant visiting school assemblies, preaching the value of enthusiasm and skill and being good at *something*.

Mark wondered. *Does this qualify? Or could we all get suspended?* Nowadays, there was often a blurry boundary between avid self-expression and something that deserved *zero-tolerance*.

"Watch out below!" A hoarse whisper floated down from the bell tower, just ahead of a coiled end of rope. True to his promise, Tang was up there in no time. Mark admitted to himself: *impressive.* While Ricardo clamped in with his harness, Mark hoped that Barry remembered how to tie off and belay without an autotensioner. *Maybe I should have gone up to handle it.*

Maybe I should now.

But 'Cardo was already inside the niche, wedging his back against one side while bracing his climbing shoes against the other, shifting one foot and then the other as he wormed his way upward along both gritty surfaces.

Mark looked closely at the wall, ready to call a halt if the surface looked damaged — one sure way to turn a "harmless stunt" into hooligan vandalism. But it seemed to be good 'crete, not crumbly stucco. There were no scars, even when 'Cardo scuffed hard.

Backing out to look around, Mark checked for anyone passing by. Mr. Perez, the campus patrolman who took the Monday shift, would be on duty until six. But the retired cop was so preoccupied, watching every move the carnies made, that he ought to be busy down at the athletic field for a while.

Then, Mark felt a nudge on his arm. He turned ... Alex gestured with her thumb. The big, bearded carny had apparently followed them, finding a new wall to lean against while watching the climbers.

This time, the fellow's heavy eyebrows lifted slightly, accompanying the slightest nod. And Mark took the evident meaning.

Don't mind me. Just watching. I won't tell. And Mark nodded back. The carny seemed an unlikely tattle-tale.

Turning back to the business at-hand, Mark noted that 'Cardo was moving pretty quickly. Not too surprising, given his strength and small, wiry frame. He was arching and wriggling and then arching again, driving himself upward in a repetitive rhythm that would never work in a real rock chimney, with countless jagged variations and tricky surfaces that required careful evaluation and planning. *Typical X-stuff,* Mark figured. For all of their bravado, these urban adventurers relied on the predictable smoothness of their skateboard half-pipes and metro streets. None of nature's wild unpredictability for them!

"Move it, Bam," Alex said, pushing past Mark and tossing her sweatshirt at him, as Ricardo neared the top. "Use your slot or lose it."

Dang, girl, he thought. *What'd I do to you?*

Violating proper procedure, Alex started bracing herself in before 'Cardo even made it over the balcony ledge. Of course, the chances of 'Cardo falling onto her were small, given a decent belay. Still.

"Almost ... there ..." Ricardo announced, and fumbled for the chisel in his pocket. Mark watched the process warily, positioning himself in case the boy dropped his tool. If it plummeted toward Alex, Mark would have just a split second to knock it aside. *This is stupid. You don't rush things. Not even in a dopey little stunt.*

Alex seemed oblivious to any danger ... or to a sprinkle of concrete shavings that floated down, as 'Cardo carved a quick pair of initials into his chosen spot under the cornice ledge, visible only to those who would follow their path, in coming years. Hardly a case of immoral "vandalism". But if that chisel fell toward Alex —

Mark braced himself, anxiously ready to swat it out of space ...

... till 'Cardo Chavez grunted with satisfaction, twirled the tool, and jabbed it hard into a wooden eave, leaving it for the next person. Pretty deep. Mark relaxed a little.

"Gritty," Alex commented as she set her back and feet in place, testing her strength against both walls of the chimney. Without sleeves, the girl abraded her shoulders every time she arched her back to shimmy higher.

"You should wear this." He offered the sweatshirt and she seemed to ponder for a moment ... 'til a hoarse laugh from above announced 'Cardo's final arrival, scrambling over the rim with Barry's help, into the bell tower cupola. The rope soon tumbled down in a loop that uncoiled all the way to Alex. Forgetting any discomfort, she eagerly connected it to her harness, then took three deep breaths, as Mark checked all the connections. The moment he nodded, she started up — taking one short footstep, another, then heaving her pelvis upward and wriggling to bring her shoulders and back along ... all without ever losing contact with either side of the narrow slot.

For some people, it might seem an awkward process. But Alex made it look natural. In fact, she appeared more graceful right now than she did while just walking around ... a wry observation that made Mark smile ... and that he decided to keep to himself.

We are, each of us, many people inside.

The thought seemed to rise within his mind, as if out of nowhere. Watching Alex push her way up the chimney, Mark felt like at least a dozen different individuals.

A protective older friend, or brother, wary in case she slipped —

A comrade who was charged with guarding this little band against discovery, by keeping a lookout for anyone passing too close, while also wary about their not-very-welcome observer —

A student with a B average, who did *not* need a black mark on his record for college applications, wishing he had found the nerve to say no —

And a rebel who was sick of always being Mr. Responsible ... as if that trait ever paid off in any big way —

Plus yet another guy, stirring inside, who — almost in spite of himself — found that Alex's athletic ascent, writhing and grunting and far from feminine, nevertheless had an alluring and strangely attractive quality. A fascination to the eye, as well as to some of those damned, inconvenient hormonal drives that had lately ...

He pushed those thoughts aside, calling upon an image of Helene Shockley. There. Now that was an obsession. It felt more naturally erotic and far less confusing.

"Half of the decisions you'll make in life, son —" his father once said to Mark *"— the good choices and the bad ones, will often boil down to one thing. Picking* which *of your inner selves shall get to be in charge, at any given time."*

Mark shook his head, sharply. The whole world had been lecturing him, for months now. The last thing he needed was to get it from his own damn mind.

There was one antidote to uncomfortable thoughts. *Action.* Motion and the satisfaction of actually getting something done! So, before Alex was more than halfway up, he decided on impulse. Stepping into the niche between the bell tower and the main wall, Mark settled his back against one wall, feeling sharp grit poke through the fabric of the flannel shirt.

Well, if Alex could take it, he sure could.

Here goes. Alex will be done before I'm halfway up. They can drop me the rope at that point.

First one foot met the opposite wall and pressed hard ... then the other. It was a tighter fit for Mark than it had been for the other two, requiring more lateral force and muscle tension, but also offering him greater range of movement than 'Cardo or Alex had. *This shouldn't be too hard.* Settling in, he took a short step, wriggled his back upward, moved the other foot, and looked up.

Alex was quite a bit higher, only about two meters short of the top. Her arms and legs glistened with sweat and there were abrasion marks — scratches — from her shoulders to her elbows. She had slowed a bit, but seemed to have things under control.

Of course, strictly speaking, he shouldn't be here in the slot. Not with another climber above and no rope of his own. But it would only be the first few minutes and this really did feel pretty easy.

It *was* easy, at first. Step. Step. Arch and press with the arms. Wriggle higher. Then repeat. Step. Step. Arch and press with the arms. Wriggle higher. Then repeat. As he had expected, it was pretty mindless, without any of the tricky variety of a natural chimney. In fact, Mark soon found he was catching up with Alex. One of the less mature corners of his mind took some satisfaction. This'll show her.

Soon, the sophomore girl was in reach of 'Cardo's chisel. Setting herself solidly in place, she reached for it —

— when suddenly a sound floated upward from below and not too far away. Mark halted his writhing ascent to listen.

Footsteps on the nearby path. Someone whistling a nondescript tune.

From overheard, Mark heard Barry Tang's unmistakable, worried whisper. "Sh! Everybody quiet!"

What do I do? Mark pondered. *Drop back down, step out and try to distract whoever it is?*

Remain where I am, keeping as still as possible?

The footsteps drew nearer. The whistle, louder. Mark decided.

Hurry on up. That way, I'll be well above eye-level, even if someone glances inside the niche.

Somewhere inside, a little voice complained. This was probably the wrong choice. Still, *Alex* seemed to agree. Even as Mark shimmied higher, the girl stopped wrestling with 'Cardo's chisel and turned instead to finishing the climb, stretching out her right arm and reaching for the X boy's extended hand. Their fingers brushed, grabbed for each other, found a grip. 'Cardo started to pull her up ...

"Give her slack!" He whispered over his shoulder at Barry.

No, don't! But Mark's voice would not come. Caught in an awkward position, his chest had no room to push the words out.

'Cardo's grip on her arm did not look —

It all happened in a blur. Alex surrendered her chimney bridge, letting herself swing outward and dangle, giving 'Cardo's hold more trust than it deserved. 'Cardo groaned at the sudden weight. Alex reached with her other arm and scrambled for the lip of the balcony, where Barry was trying to help clutch at her ...

... letting go of his rope belay ....

... just an instant before Alex lost her grip and fell.

Letting out a cry as he twisted aside, Mark shot out his right hand out to grab at her, mid-plummet. He felt a crashing impact and, for an instant, Alex was actually *in his arm,* caught and held, swinging wildly as her eyes briefly met his. Mark's right shoulder felt yanked half from its socket and the other burned from pressure against the gritty wall, desperately holding them both up.

But it was only for a second. Then his hold broke. She fell away, resuming her rush to the ground. Mark let out a sob and braced himself to hear a crunching noise.

But the sound of impact came much softer than expected. Was it adrenaline or the pounding in his chest, that muffled the blow when she struck ground? Mark wriggled back into some kind of stable position and then — through speckled vision — forced himself to look down.

There was Alex. Safe, it seemed. In the arms of a burly man with wiry, tattooed shoulders and a dark, scraggly beard. The chain-smoking biker... now holding Alex as if she weighed almost nothing.

UP-CHUCK read a patch on the big fellow's denim shirt. After a moment or two, while the girl caught her breath, he slowly released Alex, depositing her on her own two feet, then scanned Mark and the other two boys, gaping down from the tower.

The fellow slowly smiled. At first it seemed a friendly expression ... that turned wry and disdaining ... followed by a dismissive snort. Then, before anyone could breathe a word of thanks, the man turned and was gone.

It took some minutes for Mark to worm his way back down the narrow chimney-niche between the tower and the main building. By that time, 'Cardo and Barry had rejoined Alex and were dabbing at her scratched shoulders with some alcohol pads. Nobody said a word. Mark wasn't even aware that he had injuries of his own, 'til Alex tugged at his shirt to wipe away streaks of blood. The garment wasn't going to be good for much more than the rag box, now.

Everybody was a bit subdued, avoiding eye-contact as they returned their climbing gear to the lock box. 'Cardo managed to quash any sense of elation over his own accomplishment, though at school tomorrow he would doubtless lead all the other X kids to see the chisel, poking into view under the eave of the bell tower. His signal of priority and a challenge to those who might follow.

Big deal, Mark pondered, sharing a final glance and nod with Alex. Perhaps neither of them would ever mention what had happened here. Or what it meant. But on his way home, he could still remember the mixed feelings and confusion. The arguments within, that should have led to different decisions. The sense of being many people, *all* of them terribly perplexed.

Maybe the Gift will be something to simplify it all. To cut through the puzzle of life and let people quickly see what's true.

If so, well, it sounded pretty cool ... and yet ...

And yet, casting his mind back to the intensity of those moments — and the look on Alex's face when she silently said thanks — Mark wasn't sure that he really regretted the confusion of growing up. Or anything at all.

10

ESSAY QUESTIONS

The Garubis were punctual. Friday morning, as Mark and his father had breakfast together, all of the world's three million broadcasting channels carried news, bulleted in two hundred languages.

The starship had changed orbits. It now kept station above North America.

"I'd better report to base," Dad said, standing up and taking his plate to the sink. Unspoken was the fact that his experimental team had the most advanced aircraft in the world, incorporating what few bits of alien technology the experts had managed to decipher in three frantic months. If something went wrong today ... well, that didn't bear much thinking.

"Stay cool, Dad," Mark said, quashing a tight feeling inside.

"You too, son." His father gave Mark's shoulder a squeeze, harder than usual, then departed. Mark loaded the dishwasher, hoisted his backpack and locked the front door before hopping on his bike.

Students were converging for the last day of school before Desert Carnival, but there was none of the usual chatter about who was taking whom to the dance. By the bike racks, and then on the steps leading inside, few people spoke. Dozens of guys flexed bare forearms where pixel tattoos showed the latest news reports... that a disk had once again spun off the giant cylinder in space. Another lander was leaving a trail of hot, ionized flame as it circled Earth once on its way down.

In New York, fresh preparations were underway. Perhaps this time the visitors would choose to talk a bit, when they delivered Earth's "compensation." Nobody — not even the most optimistic — expected much of a party.

Settling into his first class of the day, Mark knew that Mr. Castro had scored a bulls-eye. The topic he assigned on Monday was atop everybody's mind.

The Gift.

"What would *I* ask for?" Dave McCarty groused bitterly. "Why bother thinking about it? They don't plan to ask us what *we* want, obviously. They'll pick something *they* think we need, like grandma sending me hippie clothes every birthday."

Paulina Isfahani raised her hand.

"I'm hoping they'll offer us a better, faster way to grow meat without killing animals! We could feed the world with a lot less waste and pain." It was an old topic and getting solved already by human tech, but not fast enough for "Gaia Carers" like Paulina. She met the groans of her classmates with defiance. "I'm not surprised they weren't polite to us. We're murderers!"

Mr. Castro quashed further moans, raising both hands. "That's a legitimate hypothesis, Paulina. Any other ideas?"

Jennifer Ledgerwood spoke up, glaring at her ex-boyfriend across the aisle. "How about giving everybody a really good lie detector!"

"Hm, yes," the teacher mused. "That would certainly change politics and commerce ... as well as dating. We could discuss that one for a year. Anyone else?"

A rapid series of suggestions burst forth as each student, in turn, seemed to have a special wish.

"Flying cars!"

"Cures for disease and getting old."

"A way to learn stuff without going to school!"

"Something about God?"

"Clean energy."

"I'm hoping for some new cuisine!" announced Patrick Sauvel. "I am so sick of pizza and burgers and tacos and mu shu lo mein. Something really alien and yummy would be nice."

After the laughter died down, Lance Ford had a different suggestion.

"How about a way to, you know, freeze people and thaw them later safely? So they could be fixed when a cure is found for their sickness? Or even if you're *not* sick. You could use it to visit other planets. Or the future, where things'll be better. I bet the Garubis have that, or they couldn't go to the stars."

Some classmates nodded at this logic, but Mark knew the last part was wrong. These aliens didn't need suspended animation. They had faster-than-light transport — *much* faster — in order to have come for Na-bistaka just ten days after being called.

"Do you think people would do that?" Mr. Castro asked, clearly intrigued. "Would healthy folks have themselves frozen in order to sleep out the next century, hoping things will get better? Yes, Arlene?"

The immigrant girl lowered her hand.

"That could be the *only* way to make things better."

"What do you mean?"

"I mean that right now the world's population is so high ... it takes all of our resources just to feed people and stay even. I heard one expert predict that we'll have a 'population correction' soon. He seemed so *calm,* talking about how that would bring things back into balance, though a 'correction' like that means two or three billion people dying!"

Arlene turned to look back at the rest of the class.

"Believe me, those billions won't go willingly or peacefully! They will take the rest of us down with them."

Students stared. Nobody had never seen Arlene get so intense.

"Whereas, if we had hibernation —" Mr. Castro prompted, urging her to complete the thought.

"Well ... if such a technique proved safe and easy and cheap enough ... those same billions of people might *choose* to get out of the way, calmly sleeping and waiting it out. Meanwhile, others could use the new sup ... srup ..."

"Surplus?"

"Yes, *surplus*. Those who stay awake would have to promise to use the surplus this created, to solve problems! Invest in new cities and technologies. Clean up the environment. Make a paradise for the sleepers to wake into!"

Mark couldn't help blinking in wonder. Arlene's growing confidence had burst through some inner threshold. From a shy immigrant kid speaking broken English, she was turning into a strong person with formidable views ... if somewhat unnerving ones.

Mr. Castro mused. "I think I once read a story about that very scenario."

More groans. Ever since the world turned upside down that fateful Thursday, he kept recalling 'classic' science fiction tales about First Contact. Their variety appeared limitless, in film or book or magazine, and Mr. Castro seemed to know them all.

"I think it was written by Offutt and Lyon. Those two also wrote a scenario even more relevant to our present situation. Let me see if I can remember — I think it was about aliens who come to Earth in need of something. I don't know — maybe some chemical from daisies — it doesn't really matter.

"In this story, they offer to *buy* the thing they want, but Earth's appointed negotiator acts coy. So they up their offer, from a new power source all the way to a couple of used starships! World leaders want to leap at this, but the negotiator figures the visitors are eager, maybe even desperate. They really need this thing we have. He also figures that they are still offering the equivalent of glass beads.

"So he finally decides what to demand from them."

The teacher paused and Mark found himself waiting, tensely.

"Yeah?" Froggi Hayashi finally urged, voice edgy with impatience.

Mr. Castro smiled.

"The negotiator insists that the visitors say *please.*"

Froggi blinked a couple of times, as confused as his classmates.

"That's ... dumb."

"Is it?" Mr. Castro shrugged. "In the story, that one demand sends the aliens into a tizzy. They offer a dozen *new* starships. 'Anything but that,' they cry. 'Don't make us say *please!*'"

"That doesn't make sense!"

"Oh, but it does," Helene Shockley's voice murmured behind Mark. He turned to see her hand raised, jingling copper bracelets. "I think I see what the author was getting at."

Mark saw it, too. But he had vowed to stay out of these *sci fi* discussions. Talk about aliens only churned his stomach. He wished the class would go back to ancient European History.

"You only say *please* when you talk to equals," Helene explained. "Or those close to being equal. If someone asks you 'please' for something they need, it means you get to do the same."

Then her voice dropped a little. "At least ... that's what I think the author might have meant."

Mr. Castro nodded. "That seems reasonable. Can anyone see parallels between this story and what's happening today? Mr. Bamford?"

Mark knew he would not escape by keeping silent. Still, he sighed.

"The Garubis think we're trash. That's all."

"But that's *not* all, Mark," Helene protested. "If we had *acted* like trash, they'd have felt just fine about snubbing us, or maybe doing something worse. But we surprised them."

"Maybe because our movies always show people behaving so badly," Trevor suggested. "All the TV and stuff that they watched from space ... it made them expect that we'd act a lot more stupid. A lot worse."

Helene nodded. "Maybe. Anyway, now, according to some kind of Galactic code — maybe a law or tradition — they have to treat us better than they really want to. That *means* something."

"Yeah," Mark muttered, with unexpected vehemence. "It means now they hate us. They'll hand over some booby prize and then think hard about ways to get even with us for embarrassing them. That's what lots of humans would do, admit it!"

She met his gaze. "Well ... then we just have to hope they aren't like *lots* of humans."

Again, Mark wondered if Helene was putting some kind of meaning into her words — something personal. It might be solved if he had the courage to talk to her. On the other hand, she seemed happy with her Student Body President boyfriend — they were Prom Couple — so what was there to talk about?

Maybe next year, when Scott Tepper is in college .... Is she already lining up his replacement for our senior year? Mark chewed on the thought, which tasted like a weird combination of hope, excitement and wounded pride.

Before he could reply, a low murmur intruded, growing louder outside the classroom. A mutter of human voices. It grew louder. Dave McCarty flipped open his web-unit. He, too, started babbling.

"The lander! They say it's *not* aimed for New York."

Normally, it was an infraction to open a media device in class. But not today. Mr. Castro stepped forward. "Where do they say —"

"When it passed Hawaii the trajectory seemed bound for Southern California. Mojave Desert."

Which makes it easy to guess what the precise target is, Mark realized. *The Contact Center. Those white domes at the end of a runway, where Nabistaka accepted our hospitality and every comfort we could provide.*

Dad will get a front row seat. Maybe he'll be first to see this "Gift" when they roll it out. Unless he's scrambled and airborne when it comes.

By this time the TV – an entire, pixelated wall, was on, showing one network's quick estimate of the glide path. Sure enough, it terminated just north of Joshua Tree National Monument — in the vicinity of Twenty-Nine Palms, California.

Doubtless, every helicopter in Los Angeles would be on its way here in moments, carrying frantic journalists back to their old stake-out.

When the period bell rang, some students wandered out and a few others drifted in, as if expecting the next class to begin as usual. It didn't, of course. Any semblance of a normal schedule was completely forgotten as teachers and students alike clustered around the nearest media source. That is, until a deep-throated *thunder* rattled the windows and rocked the sky, much lower and more ominous than the familiar sonic booms of US Marine Corps jets.

Suddenly, every artificial medium was abandoned. Students, teachers and staff poured outdoors, shading their eyes against the sky blue glare as sharp sunlight reflected off a disklike object, now creeping slowly from the west amid a rising growl.

Despite his cynicism, Mark found it astonishing to see a Garubis vessel up close. It made a vision far more vast and palpable than he had expected from televised images. In fact, for a minute or two he actually felt ... well ... privileged. The sheer beauty of the glistening craft — still emitting a glow from its fiery path through the atmosphere — went beyond any issue he might have with the people flying it.

Alex felt the same way.

"Something to tell the grandchildren, eh?" she said, nudging Mark as she joined him on the front steps.

"Uh huh." And yet, squinting, Mark found himself starting to worry. Something seemed wrong about the ship's slow trajectory across the sky. Something unexpected.

They were joined by Barry Tang who asked Alex. "Isn't your mother at the Contact Center?"

"Yeah. She was disappointed not to be part of the Eastern Team, but now she'll be right where the action is! Mark's father, too. We'll get first-hand stories."

"Maybe," Mark commented amid a growing concern, as he watched the lander's puzzling approach pattern. Barry saved him from having to say it aloud.

"Is it just me?" the younger boy mused. "Or does it look like that ship is —"

Slowing down a bit too much, Mark thought as Barry fell silent. *And it's not on a direct course for the air base.*

In fact, the huge flying craft did not waver a bit, left or right, as it came straight at them. From this shortened distance, that meant the lander couldn't be heading for the Contact Center, five miles to the north.

It's ... coming here.

Seconds later that fact grew obvious to everyone, as a door opened in the side of the great disk, vomiting a cloud of cylindrical drones that came swooping toward the town. This time, everyone knew about the Garubis style of landing. But it was one thing to watch on TV and quite another for the flurry of hollow tubes to hurtle *toward you,* like a swarm of huge, angry bees.

People screamed. Quite a few started to run, but the whirling cyclone of flying things now surrounded a few city blocks. It took more courage to approach the perimeter than to retreat inside the school.

Even from a height of a thousand feet, exhaust blasting down from the hovering lander felt uncomfortably hot. Only a hardy minority of students and staff remained outside to watch three spindly-but-massive legs rapidly take shape, self-assembling and climbing swiftly into the sky. One pillar slanted upward from just beyond the Food King's far parking lot. A second crushed a hapless semi-trailer to bits, next to the Shell station. The third spire set carnival dogs yelping madly as it grew upward from the athletic field.

"I guess —" Barry stammered. "I g-guess they're gonna give the ... the Gift to —"

"— to *us.*" Alex finished the thought for him. "Damn. It better be something cool."

Speaking of cool, Mark admired how Alex was keeping hers. Then he caught her glancing up at him and realized. *She thinks the same thing about me.*

A completely different sound made him swivel as — with a theatrical vroom — a white van tore along Rimpau Avenue, plunging through the swirl of alien drones, miraculously colliding with none of them. Barreling along the street, it pulled up, amid squealing brakes, before the high school. At first, Mark thought it might be science types from Cirocco Labs, because the vehicle bore an array of dishes and antennas on its roof. But no. Out piled the reporter from Channel Six — *Headwitness News* – and her faithful tech-cameraman.

Up and down Rimpau, he glimpsed similar enthusiasts, attempting to brave that cyclone of drone cylinders. Some students tried to flee the looming "gift" delivery, while other daring folks from town tried just as hard to get in. Six local bikers weaved confidently inward, seeking the eye of the storm.

But for most there was no time to try, or even decide. Barely more than a minute after it began, the tripod was finished self-assembling and the lander was settling quickly into place, at least two hundred meters overhead. The blast of warm air tapered off and then ceased

...

... but not a low hum that seemed to vibrate his very innards.

Now that the razor cloud of intimidating cylinder-drones was gone, more people moved. A few ran for the perimeter — Mark noticed Tom Spencer, not hanging around to see what his reward might be for rescuing a stranded creature from the desert sands. Others hurried forward, scooting in from the town, driven more by excitement than fear.

Go or stay? he asked himself, as the vibration seemed to intensify, plucking his bones like strings. Mark knew, somehow, that Alex and Barry would follow, whatever he chose to do.

Decide now.

11

PARENTAL NOTIFICATION

Rushing from the white dome of the Contact Center, Dr. Karen Polandres-Behr flashed her credentials and commandeered a place aboard one of the helicopters rising from the nearby airstrip. Voices yammered frantic questions in her ear via a secure link to other members of her team, assembled in New York.

"I don't know anything yet!" she shouted as the chopper pilot set blades spinning. "The tripod stands just south of here, right over the town! No, we haven't heard a peep from the lander. Has there been anything from the Mother Ship?"

"Nothing at all."

Lifting off, the copter soon gave her a better perspective. The alien tower-platform had seemed impressive last Saturday, standing beside Manhattan's skyscrapers. Now, above the open desert, it resembled a mountain, a stool for gods, a giant *fork* stuck in the Earth. Air force planes and news copters buzzing nearby only drove home the scale of the thing. They were mosquitoes. Less than mosquitoes.

"Oh dear lord," she murmured as they gained enough altitude to look down — at an angle — upon the little city of Twenty-Nine Palms. "It's standing right over my daughter's school."

The helicopter pitched and bucked.

"Keep it still!" One of Karen's associates demanded, trying to aim instruments at the spacecraft. It was doing something — manipulating mighty forces. The detector device on her lap told her that much, before every dial went into redline, reached its max value or simply burned out.

"Something's screwing the electronics," the pilot snapped. Karen noticed several cockpit meters twitching to the same rhythm of static she heard in her headset, a rhythm that seemed also to penetrate her skin.

Despite the noise, New York kept hurling frantic questions.

"I don't know!" She repeated. "But I think something's about to happen!"

More frenzied queries rattled her ears, but she could only answer with a low cry as the Garubis lander shuddered, causing the tripod to tremble visibly. It changed *color* before her eyes, sliding along the spectrum from reddish toward yellow, green and finally intense blue.

Then, from the vessel's rim, there fell a curtain of dazzling light, dripping slowly as if liquid.

In terrified dismay, Karen saw the radiant cone broaden — catching two nearby earthling aircraft in its hem, melting their rotors and tossing them like gnats, sending them a-tumble toward the Mojave dunes. Then the curtain tightened inward, narrowing to fit snugly within the trio of legs. It was hard to peer at the fierce illumination, which seemed to solidify somehow, into a bubble of palpable brilliance.

A jolt shook the chopper. The pilot struggled, throwing his throttle to full and climbing even as a shock wave — visible as a ripple in the air — caught up and plowed into them. Roaring, dazzling brilliance heaved around her. Karen held on for dear life as the helicopter dipped, rattled and shook. Alarms wailed. The control panel erupted with red lights. Technicians protected precious instruments with their bodies.

For a minute, it seemed all was lost. Next stop, the hard Earth.

Then, abruptly, the sensation of powerful energies simply

vanished. In seconds the air calmed, releasing her pilot to sob in relief. And Karen's head was out the door, turning and peering frantically.

The first thing she saw was a pillar of smoke rising from flaming wreckage — an aircraft, probably one of the experimental fighter planes, lay in a crumpled heap at one end of a city street, with a trail of torn autos in its wake. That was awful enough. But she wasted no time turning the other way, to find —

— a pall of sparkling dust hanging over the part of town near Olympic and Rimpau, obscuring everything beneath. Out of this fog, the last few bits and flying components of the landing tripod could be seen rushing skyward, joining their fellows in the belly of the giant, hovering disk. Soon they were all recovered and the big hatch closed.

The great vessel began climbing away.

"*What happened? What happened? What happened?*"

For a moment Karen could not tell where the question came from. It was almost a simultaneous chant, emitted from her headphones, from everyone in the chopper, and from her own dazzled mind.

Then, as the alien vessel started moving, an amplified voice took over the radio waves.

Thus, repayment is accomplished.
With this gift, the debt is erased.

Where the tripod had been, just minutes before, a stiffening breeze now tugged at the dust cloud, unraveling it — along with every shred of hope Karen had been vainly clutching. For under the clearing haze, she now saw that the whole area now lay empty.

Worse than empty.

The high school and several city blocks... were gone! Just a crater remained, circular, smooth-sided, and uniformly several meters deep.

A quiet, crystal clarity settled upon Karen's senses. Over headphones she heard someone in authority shout a protest that was immediately translated into Garubis chatter-gabble as it chased after the fast-departing vessel.

"You ugly alien bastards! You call THIS a gift?"

The answer came almost immediately.

It is more than adequate, chosen from the
Wish List for Ambitious Upstarts.

Now we can wipe our feet clean of your dross.
When we next meet, it will be without a burden of debt.
On our terms.

Earth's spokesman retorted in anger, speaking for a shocked human race.

"This meeting isn't over, you sons of bitches. Nobody disintegrates our kids and gets away with it!"

Glittering reflections off metal. Angry jets converging, racing, kicked in their afterburners to catch up with the fast-receding alien craft ... but Karen saw it was hopeless. All the fighter planes could do was launch a few missiles that streaked vengefully after the Garubis disk, then fell away as the vessel accelerated blithely, indifferently, toward space.

Karen had already dismissed the idea of revenge, at least for now. Tomorrow there would be work to do, analyzing what weapon had done this thing, and beginning the hard process of arming humankind for life in a hostile universe. A cosmos where the rules of "debt" and "honor" were apparently far weirder than any Earthling had formerly imagined.

One where slaying a thousand adolescents was 'repayment' for an act of hospitality.

For now though, all she could do was stare at the steaming crater — its smooth floor now stained with liquids pouring from severed utility pipes. Water. Gasoline. Sewage. Soon, sparks from a broken electric line set the puddles ablaze.

Karen felt certain that she could put out the flames with her tears.

12

FIELD TRIP

A pall of dust filled the air, obscuring all sight of the towering tripod, the Garubis vessel ... or the sky.

Even if the way had been clear, Mark wouldn't have seen much. Like everyone else, he was overwhelmed with nausea that lasted for several ...

... seconds?

... minutes?

Something told him the confusion had stretched longer than that. Much longer — during the span between two breaths — while that brilliant, mind-numbing curtain poured down from the alien craft, tightening and coiling around them all ...

What — he thought, feeling his chest heave for the next precious gasp of air.

When it finally came, with a wrenching half-sob, another shock hit him from a different place — his nasal cavities.

Smell!

Make that *smells*. A flood of unfamiliar aromas. Pungent, lush, sweet, tart, acrid, fatty, musty, fruity, reeking — and yet *none* of those things. There were strangenesses — frightening and intoxicating — in the very wind.

That was the first hint. Before Mark's eyes could see or the ringing left his ears, an ancient portion of his brain knew, from smell alone. Something had changed, far more than a mere dust cloud.

What is it? Have they decided to kill us?

If they had a beef, shouldn't it be with me ... not with everyone at the school?

Determined to face it like a man, Mark forced his spine erect, waving away still-swirling puffs and blinking hard in order to clear away the spots. Lifting his face skyward in defiance, he raised a hand to shade his eyes ...

... and saw nothing overhead but dissipating haze ... and then clouds, rolling slowly across a blue sky.

The Garubis were gone, vanished, without a trace.

But it was the *shade* of blue overhead that unnerved him more than anything else. That, combined with the persistent, exotic aromas. Mark felt a chill climb his back as he lowered his gaze.

The murk began to clear.

"No," he sighed as shapes emerged.

Behind him stood the solid, reassuring bulk of Twenty-Nine Palms High School, with its broad front steps beneath his feet. Nearby, Alex, Barry and several dozen other students were gathering themselves after waves of nausea similar to his own. Further, beyond a stretch of lawn and a precariously tilting flag pole, stood Rimpau Avenue, a row of teetering palm trees, then the Food King.

That is — half of Food King. Where the rest of the supermarket should have been, a wall of *forest* now stood. Trees wew familiar in their pattern of branching limbs, but not in the wild colors of their leaves – crimson-tipped and lime. The nearest swayed and rippled from some recent disturbance. Several toppled over and crashed before Mark's unbelieving eyes.

"Are ..." Mark swallowed. "Are you all right?" he asked Alexandra and Barry, helping them steady themselves, even as he turned to survey the forest verge. It swept in a perfect arc along one wall of the minimart, slicing Drannen's Hardware down the middle, then continued through Marshall Motors where one row of cars had been reduced to steaming fragments.

"I think so," Alex answered. Barry gave a jerky nod, staring wide-eyed.

"Good. Come on then."

Mark started at a walk, as his friends recovered their balance. But in seconds it became a jog. Alex kept pace alongside as Mark went faster down the street, heading toward the nearest edge, feeling a sudden need to hurry. They took the last fifty meters at a run over cracked pavement, past a BMW with its alarm blaring, only stopping when they reached the rim of a sheer, five-meter drop. There, they stared down at an injured meadow that hissed and groaned in complaint.

Well, you'd feel wounded too, if someone dropped part of an American town on top of you, he thought, numbly.

One surviving tree pushed a clumpy spray of multicolored leaves near enough to touch. He reached toward it.

"Careful," Alex said. "All of this may be poisonous." She gestured at the forest, the clearings, and expanse of rolling hills that now lay before them.

Mark quashed a sudden, hysterical urge to laugh. Somehow, he doubted the Garubis would go to all this trouble if the dangers were so simple or instantly overwhelming here. Wherever *here* was.

Oh, there were perils, almost certainly. But Na-bistaka's folk operated according to some kind of code, one that limited their viciousness. There would be a chance, if a slim one.

Out of stunned silence, a babble began to rise. *Two* babbles, actually. One ahead of him, as the forest began stirring again. No animal had yet shown itself, but he could hear local creatures rustling, getting over their panic and surprise as a chunk of Planet Earth plopped into their rustic paradise.

But a louder clamor came from behind — the loud and unreserved voices of Americans, who had never learned — till now — any of the arts of prudence. How or when to be quiet. They came spilling out of the High School and other places of shelter, staring at the off-blue sky, the strangely too-yellow sun, the circle of gaudy forest and a range of snow-capped, serrated mountains that could be seen rising in the distance, far beyond the truncated athletic field.

"They sent us to some faraway planet!" Barry murmured. "They promised us a gift. Instead they *punished* us!"

"No." Alex shook her head, pausing a moment, staring at the beautiful strangeness. When she next spoke, her voice was hoarse but clear. "They may be spiteful devils, who should fry over a spit, but you *can* call this a gift."

When Mark grunted in agreement, Barry cast him a questioning look.

"A colony," he explained, unable to utter more.

"C-colony?"

"Another world for humanity," Alex summed up, "if we manage to survive."

"A colony," Mark said again, letting the word sink in, and realizing that — crazy as it sounded — it must be true.

"Of course, they might've *told* us!" Alex murmured bitterly

Mark nodded. No kidding.

Given six days warning, a nation and world could have organized any number of volunteers, sorted by skill and profession, outfitted with every tool, ready for any contingency. Just a little advance notice would have allowed humanity a chance to gather its brightest and best-trained adults, ready to create a sturdy and technologically prepared settlement. One equipped to study a new world, to come to terms with it, and to thrive.

But the Garubis didn't give notice. Instead, those arrogant space-jerks, without warning, chose to transport —

He looked around at his companions-in-exile. A thousand California teenagers, a hundred or so teachers and townsfolk, some carnival workers, a bag lady or two, all of them wandering in a fog of confusion and disbelief.

It's a gift. Chosen from that 'list' they mentioned, because some law or tradition required that they repay a debt they owed.

They had to give us something valuable ...

... but they twisted the rules.

Na-Bistaka — that nasty — must have done this as a joke, certain that we'll fail.

And we may fail. We may.

His jaw clenched hard.

But not if I have anything to say about it.

Mark turned to Alexandra, who looked very young and yet somehow steadier than any of the adults who could be seen right now, babbling in the street.

"We better hurry," he said. "There's a lot to do."

HE SAID THE WORDS, but it was Alexandra Behr who proved herself quick and resourceful, during those first crucial seconds on a new world. Mark still felt a bit dazzled by just how quick.

Their slab of Earth – torn out by advanced alien science-magic – must have popped into space just above the forest, because everyone felt a sense of falling several meters, maybe farther. The air still vibrated from the painful thud that followed, as the dazzling, force-field curtain evaporated ... when Alex seemed to grasp their situation before anyone else.

Oh, sure, it was Mark who led a group of teens rushing toward the edge, to gaze out over the crushed and trembling red-green vegetation below. But while Mark only gawked at the strange forest, Alex shouted— "It's spilling!"

She jabbed Mark and Barry Tang, shaking them out of dumb paralysis. "We gotta catch it!" Alex cried, pointing.

Streams of pale fluid poured from three closely-grouped pipes a few meters below the edge of the disk. Pungent liquid splattered across alien trees. *Gasoline,* Mark understood an eye-blink later, desperately trying to wake himself from shock.

Jonathan's Shell Station once featured two double-islands of pumps. Now the tarmac ended where the second group belonged. Worse, this slice of Earth was too unstable to hold the station's underground tanks — not intact. Depending on breaks and leaks, there might be an almost-full chamber... or perhaps not be any gasoline left except what was burbling out of these severed pipes. That made it as valuable as blood.

Alex was a junior like Mark, though she had yet to reach her sixteenth birthday. Still coltish—and she was a ball of fire. "Grab buckets, tubs, anything!" Alex jerked her thumb at the school. "You try the janitor's room! I'll look over here!" That last part was shouted over her shoulder as she charged toward the ruins of Drannen's Hardware.

Barry and most of the others went running, so Mark stayed put, pretty sure that he knew what Alex was planning. He leaned out over the fifteen-foot cliff, glancing sideways at the street.

The water and sewer mains must have been cut, too. *What else?* he thought. *There must be a natural gas line, and phone and fiber optic cables* ... Those didn't seem urgent. But was there any way to cap the water main before it all ran out? How many places would need to be plugged all around the island? *Man ... look at all the underground crap we took for granted!*

Mark paced away from the gas pipes toward the wide street, but he couldn't see or hear anything spilling out from under the road. *Maybe there's already no water left except what's in toilet tanks and water heaters ... a few stretches of plumbing here and there ...*

Or maybe their island tilted slightly the other way. He couldn't tell; the Disk was too big. But if so, the severed water mains would be emptying out on the far edge behind him.

There's no time. Choose. You have to choose.

Mark hurried back to the crumbling edge and tested the surface, seeking a way down. A slip would be very bad. The crushed mat of vegetation might break a fall, but even if it wasn't toxic on contact, he didn't want to land on top of a giant Venus flytrap or an angry, alien snake-thing. Whatever they had on this planet

Asphalt broke off as chunks in his hands. Then the gravel pack beneath spilled away as Mark dug for purchase with his cross-train-ers. Below that, fortunately, lay some good hard Mojave Desert earth, shot through with a mesh of hardy roots, great for handholds. The mulberry trees that had lined the Shell station weren't native to southern California, like so much of the inappropriate landscaping that businesses and homeowners imported, but right now he was glad for those roots. *Anyway, 'native' has taken a whole different meaning...*

The smell of gasoline was strong as he descended. Probably a huge wave of it had splashed out of a cracked storage tank. Mark found the aroma weirdly invigorating, even if the fumes were dangerous. They made his head swim and he wondered if the air mixture might be flammable, even explosive. Still, it was a city smell, an *Earth* smell, fighting the weird, acidic stink of the jungle.

Almost there, he thought, using two iffy footholds and one of the thickest roots to hang on the short face of the cliff. The pipes were about a meter and a half below the tarmac and this slab of Twenty-Nine Palms only extended another three or four beneath the pipes, with piles of rubble and smashed red plants reaching halfway up in places.

If a ten-eyed purple lion with octopus arms jumped out of those bushes, Mark wouldn't have much warning.

This was a bad idea, he thought, gritting his teeth.

Then Alex and Barry were back, standing above him with a few buckets. Other kids arrived with their arms full of paint trays that were nearly useless as containers. Best of all, Alex brought some rope. It snaked down to Mark, who used one hand to whip it into a simple support bowline. There was no time for anything fancy.

"Wait!" Alex called. "Got to tie off." She ran to secure the other end, maybe to the remaining gas pumps.

Meanwhile, Barry grimaced down past Mark. "Let's hope those other guys have better luck. Half the hardware store is *gone*, Mark, I mean just gone, like even part of a box of screws was just laying there cut in half. Cut *perfectly* in half, like a laser went through it, like we were all *inside* a laser."

Barry babbled ... though actually, he seemed better off than anyone might expect. Still, Mark was glad when Alex returned and shouldered the black-haired sophomore aside. "Bamford, are you stupid?" she yelled. "You should have waited till we could belay!"

A senior named Charlie Escobar got back with four plastic trash-cans. "What are you guys doing?" Charlie shouted. "Hurry up! It's barely a trickle already!"

"Do *you* want to try it?" Alex said.

"*Jump*, dude!" Charlie shouted. "Get on the ground and we'll throw you the—"

"No! Just ... give me a second," Mark said. "Okay, now pass me some of those smaller cans. And get more rope to tie on to the other ones!"

"We can fit the cans in these shopping baskets," Barry said. "We'll use 'em to haul the cans up and down."

"Go find more rope," Alex said to Charlie. "Please."

"Yeah. All right." Charlie cast one more frown over the edge, then sprinted away, shouting. Mark tested the crude harness under his armpits, then called, "Belay on!"

"On belay," Alex answered.

Mark never hesitated as he put his weight – maybe his life — into her hands. He got himself down alongside the pipes in an instant, dug his shoes into the rough face of dirt and leaned back, spreading his arms to catch a plastic trashcan from Barry.

It whacked him in the jaw.

"Ooof!" No problem. He fumbled and pushed it under the streaming gas.

The fluid came in belches as it squeezed out past bubbles of air. Luckily, the impact must have bent the three pipes upward and badly kinked two of them as well, slowing the flow of premium, mid-grade and regular.

Mark didn't even try to keep the octanes separate. *Just save as much as possible.* He guessed he had four gallons before the small trashcan grew hard to handle. It was less than half full but he couldn't hold more weight, hanging there on his toes. He hollered, "Okay, Barry. Haul away!"

They lowered a yellow plastic shopping basket on two lines. Mark tried to plunk the trashcan down into it, but he lost too much of his precious load when the basket swayed and he tottered out from the wall of dirt, hearing everyone shout.

They got better. Barry's basket-elevator was smart stuff. The next bucket swap was more efficient.

Alex screamed at someone: "Get away you idiots!" And Mark glanced up to see her push at a pair – a man and a woman – who were laying on their bellies at the edge, trying to push a camera and microphone down at Mark! He ignored the fools and kept working, as Alex kicked at them, until they went away.

Soon it became like an assembly line. "Faster!" Mark yelled, trying to hold two buckets at once. The rich amber gasoline was barely dribbling now. *We can siphon from cars*, he thought. What else? The carnival trucks. *There's probably still some gas caught in those pumps, too, but that'll be the only—*

"Now you," Barry said. "Mark? Now you!" Barry waved for him to climb, and Mark could hear Alex's voice rising somewhere above him. The last bucket of gas had already gone up, but instead of climbing after it, Mark twisted around to look out at the eerie red-and-gold jungle.

Maybe it was fatigue, or dizziness from the fumes. Somehow he felt unnaturally calm, hanging there on a thread, halfway between Earth and another world.

Our world, he thought. *Even if the aliens change their minds... or this is some kind of test... or rescue comes ... or if someday we find a way back ... Right now we have to act like this place is home now. Forever.*

The truth of it felt massive. Terrifying. Mark was sore and tired. And he stank. Every scrape on his hands stung from the gasoline. A bruised elbow throbbed. Yet he felt good. He almost untied and hopped down, overcome by the temptation to be the first human being to actually touch this strange world. The impulse felt as real as his breath.

He was so close. He could actually make out veins in the leaves of a nearby tree, where photosynthesis must work differently than back home. He knew that much from biology class.

Chlorophyll was green, so these plants must use something else …

"Get him up!" Alex was very loud now and Mark's harness tightened uncomfortably. She was pulling. Then the line jerked. Other kids must have added their hands to the rope, too. Mark had no choice. He turned back to the wall of dirt and moved his legs, though they felt miles away, climb-walking upward to keep from being dragged over pipes and ragged asphalt.

Still, his head just wouldn't let go of the temptation, ringing with mixed feelings of loss and distance and newness. He wanted to jump down!

Well, I guess that was one small step for a man, he thought, remembering old, x-tube immersions Dad had shown him of the Apollo XI moon landing.

Thinking of his father caused bright, lonely pangs of heartache. At the same time, Mark knew in his bones — Dad would be both proud and envious of him. Because this was an opportunity like no other. Heck, almost anything that a person did here today might turn out to be *history* in the making. If humans survived on this world and made a go of it, that is.

We'll see, he thought as he reached the rim and felt the strong grip of his friends, hauling him the rest of the way, back onto the slab of Earth. *We'll see if it's any kind of a leap for mankind.*

THE HOURS that followed were hectic. Nonstop, frantic work until …

… until suddenly there came a breather. A moment to climb up to the High School's bell tower and have a good look around. To see what had been accomplished.

Not enough, he thought. *We haven't done nearly enough.*

From atop the High School's mission-style bell tower, Mark stared across Rimpau Avenue and the smoldering ruins of the Shell station, past a sudden, curving precipice to a sweeping vale of alien forest. Some miles beyond the red-and-lime jungle, there jutted a line of sheer, almost-glassy, purple cliffs, a high ridge of iridescent stone that slanted away toward serried ranges of serrated mountains.

In the opposite direction – which the Physics Club guys were now calling North – a rolling landscape, dotted with meadows, sank gradually into a far-off haze that might hint at a much larger shoreline, perhaps even a sea.

We're not in California anymore, he thought.

All things considered, I'd rather be in Kansas.

From this height, there was no mistaking what had happened to the school and a few nearby city blocks. Perhaps that was why only a couple of dozen kids had come up here, yet, to feast on the full view. Most of the castaways – even those who were keeping busy at urgent tasks — kept gazing downward at familiar things, like a small patch of pavement, avoiding the truth while stumbling in a half-daze — or worse. Hours after a traumatic *snatch,* almost a hundred students were still cowering in dim classrooms with the blinds drawn. Not good prospects to recruit for lookout duty.

Fortunately, people came in all kinds. Some took the word "adaptable" even farther than Mark. Farther than sane, perhaps.

"Howzit, Bam?" asked the boy who had been keeping watch in the tower. He wore a wide-brimmed gray hat swiped from the janitor's closet. Mark had insisted, since no one knew how fiercely this sun's light would affect human skin, but Dave McCarty was clearly happy up here, soaking in the view.

"Zit happens," Mark replied, with a shrug. "Any changes?"

Dave was into Harleys and thrash metal, but seemed perfectly okay with moving on to other interests.

"There's nothing dangerous as far as I can tell. No more trees falling over. Oh, say! I spotted five different kinds of bird-things." He opened his scroll-tablet by pulling apart the two rods, and the big screen showed Mark several blurry images of strange things fluttering or diving with four wings. Like large, feathered insects.

"I'm still deciding which of 'em to name after me."

Mark smiled grimly. "Well, don't drain your battery, It may take a while to rig something to run rechargers."

Dave was clearly loving every minute of this, and couldn't wait to make this planet his own. More power to him. That kind of personality might prove crazy, or crazy-useful, in the days ahead. Mark had closer, harsher concerns. For now, he only had attention for their tiny slice of Earth.

From fifty feet up, he could see just how much — how little — of their home town had been carved up and deposited unknown lightyears away from home — a disk less than four hundred meters across – or half a dozen football fields — and ten meters thick. Their island was just big enough to encompass most of the high school grounds, plus a few homes and small businesses, including two-thirds of the Food King.

Thank God for that last stroke of luck, he thought, walking around the top of the tower again. *And let's hope we're making the best of it.*

Dave sniffed and pulled back from him. "Dude, you absolutely reek like gasoline. Why don't you take a shower or something before you blow up?"

Mark would like nothing better, yet he shook his head. This valley was covered in jungle — the trees and underbrush looked as thick as rain forest — but there wasn't a cloud in the sky. They couldn't be sure when or if there would be a storm. And what if the downpour wasn't safe to drink? "Shouldn't waste water," Mark said.

"Water. Right. Bummer." Dave nodded. "That was some fast thinking by you and Alex, by the way. Everybody's talking about it."

Mark nodded, accepting the compliment, but wondered. *What did I really do when the noise stopped and everyone stood up ... staring around ourselves at the Great Gift that the Garubis gave us? I tried to cope, I guess ... Sometimes you don't have a second to think. You just act.*

Smoke wafted from the Food King parking lot, where a crowd of TNPHS kids tended several barbecue grills with price tags still flapping on the handles. Clumsily, and a bit dangerously, volunteers hacked away with butcher's knives, cutting everything in the supermarket's meat section, converting steaks, roasts, and whole chickens into thin strips. Others dipped the strips of meat into a salty marinade, then spread their work above smoldering charcoal.

It had taken Mark half an hour to show them how to turn raw meat into jerky that could be stored without refrigeration, at least till the castaways figured out what else there might be to eat around here. By the time others knew enough to take over the job, his exhausted, quivering arms had been covered in blood up to his elbows. But there wasn't anyone else. TNPHS had no cooking staff, not since the school switched completely to franchise food twenty years ago. *Only tomorrow there won't be any delivery trucks to refill the cafeteria or the vending machines,* he thought.

All of the supermarket's perishables began to thaw when the electricity went out. At Barry's suggestion, the very first meal served on this new world consisted of *ice cream* — as much as anybody wanted — not only to salvage the stuff before it melted, but also to give everyone a badly-needed boost. Even among the dozens of stunned teenagers who were in the worst shape, cringing in darkened rooms, praying for this calamity to go away, many seemed to rouse a bit when spoons were thrust into their hands along with a pint of Cherry Blitz or Webonanza, Beijing-Berry or Double Chocolate Chunk.

In Mark's estimate, Barry deserved some kind of medal, especially as it grew evident how varied people could be. Some who you'd least expect turned out to be pragmatic, active types. Others faltered. The imposing Chief of Campus Security, Mr. Perez, wandered around, babbling in a soft, unnerving tone, alternately stroking his bear-like pot belly or the revolver at his hip. Meanwhile, an unlikely trio of sophomore girls, previously known only for useless giggling and gossip, took charge of preparing tonight's first and final all-you-can-eat New World Burger Bash.

As for tomorrow—

Mark still felt a twinge, recalling the Food King's freezer section. As much as possible had been crammed tight, in hope of hanging on to some of the chill. But gourmet dinners and ready-to-heat pizzas were already beginning to thaw. Cheesecakes and tater tots, frozen strawberries and cans of concentrated orange juice ... No matter how many ingenious tricks they came up with, most of it would be on the verge of going bad by morning. Whenever morning came.

Among the resilient ones? About half of the science nerds. Those who had not given in to shock or panic seemed to share the very opposite reaction, plunging into a state of focus that seemed way-intense, showing the kind of teamwork they were accustomed to pouring into quiz contests and robot competitions. Just ninety minutes or so after the arrival, Mr. Davis and his physics geeks gave a preliminary report on this new planet. A simple pendulum experiment showed it had only nine-tenths the gravity of Earth, for example. Maybe that helped put a little spring into everyone's step. But there was more. The too-yellow sun moved too-slowly across the sky.

We might as well dump all our clocks over the cliff-edge. And before the next long day, there was going to be an awfully long night.

Looking down, Mark saw again the pair of fools who had tried to shove a camera and microphone down at him, when he was dangling over the edge, salvaging gas. They were from Channel Six *"Headwitness News: On The Spot News Leaders for San Bernardino County!"* So read a logo emblazoned on their van, whose now-useless roof antennas jutted skyward. The woman reporter and her technician-cameraman must have rushed to the school as soon as the Garubis ship arrived overhead. A brave or dedicated move ... and a stupid one. Now, trapped like everyone else.

Keeping busy is therapeutic for shock, Mark pondered hours later, watching them still scurrying about, poking their lenses at everyone who was busy. *And who am I to judge what's crazy.*

Dave had been looking elsewhere with his binoculars while Mark surveyed activity below. At last, Mark turned and said, "You're okay alone up here for a while longer?"

The gangly blond nodded. "It's all good, dude. Real good. I've been naming the mountains, and that river. I got everything in here." Dave held up the tubelike scroll-tablet, covered with stickers of guitars and band logos. "Think about it. Any names we lay down will stick for hundreds of years. Maybe forever!"

For Dave and a small minority like him, the *gift* of the Garubis was exactly that, something great and thrilling, a sudden immersion into a different world that just had to be better than his old life!

Dave's intoxication, the way he stared joyfully at the new shapes and colors, struck Mark as a little frantic, nor even entirely sane. But who was he to judge another guy's way of coping? Mark's own method was to keep busy – the reason he clambered all the way up here again. Looking for anything urgent they might have missed.

"Looks like they got the last of the booze," Dave said, pointing the other way.

Mark saw a caravan of shopping carts now leaving the Food King. Pushed by several of the biggest faculty, the carts were heavily laden with bottles, cases, and kegs. In front strode the tall form of Principal Jeffers, stern and capable, his priorities clear. This was their third trip to ferry all of the prescription drugs and alcohol across Rimpau and up the school steps, into Jeffers' locked office.

And so it went, a few clusters of activity organized by anyone with a plan and a loud enough voice, while others scooped dismally at tepid ice cream or just sat and stared. Or meandered aimlessly, lacking any will or focus.

"Why us?" they asked. Mark couldn't walk more than thirty feet down there without hearing that complaint. "Why did the Garubis punish us? We're just kids!"

Why ask me? As if I know?

But some of the kids seemed to think that he did. That he *had to* know something. Just because he had spoken once or twice with Na-Bistaka, the alien envoy, and ... well ... and maybe saved the unpleasant fellow's life.

One small group struck Mark as so poignant that he felt a catch in his throat when he saw them using paints from the art room to make a big sign, drawing neat letters on the other side of a banner for the never-gonna-happen Desert Carnival dance.

PLEASE. WE'RE SORRY. TAKE US HOME.

He didn't expect the appeal to do any good. Still, when they unfurled their work between two poles at the edge of the disk, turning to aim it this way and that, Mark felt his breath catch, for a full minute. As if half in expectation, or hope, that the petition might work. Because up until this very day, *fairness* really *had* been an element of daily life.

Oh, there was always bad or uneven luck, and not all injustice could be appealed, even in mellow California of the year 2028. But some of it — a lot of it — could be. Anyway, one rule of American teenage life was: *hey, what does it hurt to ask?*

When the plaintive artists finally gave up, leaving their entreaty on a patch of lawn, facing skyward, Mark noticed that nobody stepped on it or even let a shadow block it from the heavens.

Beyond twelve hundred or so students, the Rock's population included a couple of dozen faculty, and about the same number of townspeople from stores and homes surrounding the school, or unlucky enough to be driving past when the dazzling curtain fell. Plus at least twenty carnival workers who had been erecting the Ferris Wheel, the Spinning Top, and several game booths on the football field. Mark had no great hopes for exceptional usefulness from those over twenty-one. Some of them, for sure – but far from all. If anything, the average teen seemed more resilient. At least the people who weren't doing squat could see others hard at work, laboring to make the best of a crazy situation.

"What's all that noise?" Mark shaded his eyes to peer toward the ruined car dealership.

"Oh, don't sweat it," Dave said. "That's the *defense patrol*. Varsity jocks armed with shovels and crowbars, always getting spooked by something. Bunch of drama queens, if you ask me."

"Right." Mark made a mental note to see Scott Tepper and learn more. Did Scott expect this improvised militia to accomplish much against any real danger? Like if the Garubis came back and chose to mess up Earthling lives even more.

Still, watching them hurry about the perimeter in squads with makeshift spears, Mark decided he approved. Patrolling the ring-shaped border got the athletic boys — and several girls — involved in their survival, shouting hoarsely at each other as they struggled through the wreckage of buildings along the edge of the island, grabbing bits of salvage that might fall into the surrounding moat and forest. Anyway there was no telling what kind of wildlife might emerge from the jungle. Or maybe even native creatures on a higher level, clever and resentful of invaders from space.

One likely reason they were shouting? Because very few of the gadgets that Generation M considered their birthright were any good here. There was no cell tower on this tiny wafer of home, no Internet to tap, or TV or radio broadcasts. Sure, the best devices had already done a semi-intelligent sift-search and set up a basic, ad-hoc mesh. Maybe a quarter of their Q-phones, scrolls, wristies and eBees were smart enough to join the makeshift P-to-P network in creaky ways, like exchanging old-fashioned texts. The rest had become so much pretty junk. Good for snapping a picture, but little else.

A few kids had the latest thing—active-ink tattoo-phones, which they tapped and rubbed habitually, till each one gave a mournful ping and died. Rubbing the tat any more just raised an old-fashioned welt.

Someone tried launching a mini-drone, but it soon careened out of control. *Probably because there's no GPS signals and a different magnetic field. Most of our tech is dependent on shared systems that just don't exist here.*

A new kind of silence for the hypermedia generation, sinister and unreal. Mark figured he'd seen half the kids in school, even those who knew better, wasting time as they tried over and over to get a signal. To make a call.

Who knows how many thousands of hours of battery life we've lost already. Our few solar chargers could burn out from the strain. There's got to be another way.

But he had more immediate priorities, like a growling emptiness in his belly. After all these hours scurrying about ... *I haven't eaten a single bite.* There was always so much to do. Only now he felt ravenous.

"Okay, Dave. Just don't let any of your bird-things eat you," Mark said, turning to head back down into the chaos and confusion.

Ice cream, he thought. *I hope there's still some.*

~

"Don't do that again," Alex said as Mark wolfed down more Caramel Almond Fudge in front of the Food King.

"Um." Mark felt queasy from so much sugar and fat hitting his system after a strenuous day, but he spooned up more. Better get calories.

Alex leaned over and rapped her knuckle on one of his, hard.

"Ow! *Dang.* What'd I do?"

"That business at the edge, starting descent over a loose surface without setting a belay. Don't scare me like that again, Bamford." Her brown eyes swept his face. So serious, it made her seem older –

Mark looked away first. Unconsciously or accidentally, his gaze happened across Helene Shockley, standing with Scott Tepper at the school steps.

Student body president and the varsity team quarterback, a natural at everything he does... and good-looking to boot. Of course he was named to the Emergency Committee, thrown together by Principal Jeffers. While Mark and his friends struggled to save fuel, salvage food and set up lookouts, others had been positioning themselves politically.

Helene, looking sultry and amazonic, like a candidate for Queen of the World, stood poised on the stairs with her chin up, firmly guarding access to Scott ... as Mark had discovered minutes ago when he sought information about the Defense Patrol. Rumored reports told of rabbit- and pig-sized animals scurrying in the brush — native life was returning to the area. And lately, folks increasingly had to shoo away several kinds of flying bugs, large and slow, but persistent, with iridescent wings. They left a pungent pulp when you swatted them and some kids were developing rashes. Mark had wanted to ask – was there a *policy* about killing local life forms? And had anyone thought of getting samples to the biology lab?

But Helene's protective exclusion zone was firm – reinforced with that dazzling-friendly smile. Sorry, but you only got to see Scott if you were on one of the committees sanctioned by Principal Jeffers.

Like the one building latrines – "poop decks" that stuck out over the edge of the Rock, so that waste went into the surrounding ravine – Mark wondered what the natives were making of that. It kept the shop guys busy, though, and showed that other folks were coming up with good ideas.

Or the committee working to inventory toilet paper and sanitary napkins. Or one that was acting on Alex's idea – *did they remember who suggested it?* — sending volunteers around to seal and tape closed any toilets that still had water in a tank, so that some absent-minded student wouldn't flush the precious fluid away. Barry Tang had joined the group scrounging solar chargers and getting them busy on the most essential items.

As for the vital Food Committee, none of its members had participated in the jerky-making ordeal – though they happily seized the resulting piles of dried meat and locked it all away in the Food King. Where they now roamed, scanning product codes and tabulating spreadsheets. Useful? Sure ... if completely forgetful of the roles that Mark and Alex and the Rayner girls had played.

Well, Dad warned me — *bureaucracy seldom rewards those who get stuff done.*

Helene's dazzling smile had been compensation – but only a little — for the sting of being turned away. Patronized. Ignored.

Don't stare, he reminded himself and turned his gaze away from Helene, only to catch Alex watching him. She opened her mouth, closed it, then held out a mostly-empty half-gallon container of Vanilla Bean. Mark nodded, trading her. He didn't need to ever see Caramel Almond Fudge again in his life. *And I probably won't.*

"We're buds, right?" Alex asked.

Mark felt an odd reluctance. *We're more than that. If I ever had a sister, I'd want it to be you. I'll guard you with my life. You've already saved mine a couple of times.*

But he didn't know how to say any of that. Not aloud. So he bobbed his head.

"Buds don't let buds be idiots," Alex said as she rapped him again, much softer this time. And they both managed to laugh. Only then did she add, "You don't have to kill yourself being a superstar just because you think this is all your fault, Bam."

"What? I don't ..."

He stopped.

She's right. It drives me. I do feel like I'm to blame for everyone being here. If I hadn't brought in grown-ups – NASA and the Air Force and Cirocco and the others — to rescue Na-Bistaka, Colin would've taken the alien to L.A. and it probably would have quietly faded away there. A curiosity to be poked at, till it died. Thanks to me, the whole world got involved and saved Na-Bistaka, which is why the Garubis "rewarded" us like this.

Some reward.

Still, he shook his head. "That's not it," he lied.

"Well then, whatever the reason," Alex said, and Mark thought he saw her glance at Helene ... reading him like a book. "Be smart, okay?"

He nodded, but within, he knew a deeper problem.

Once everyone has a little time to work it out, what will they say? Or do to me?

Should I be thinking about what the heck to do if I'm not safe here?

There's a whole world out there ... beyond the Edge.

The thought was about ninety percent terrifying.

And another part ... found the very notion alluring as heck.

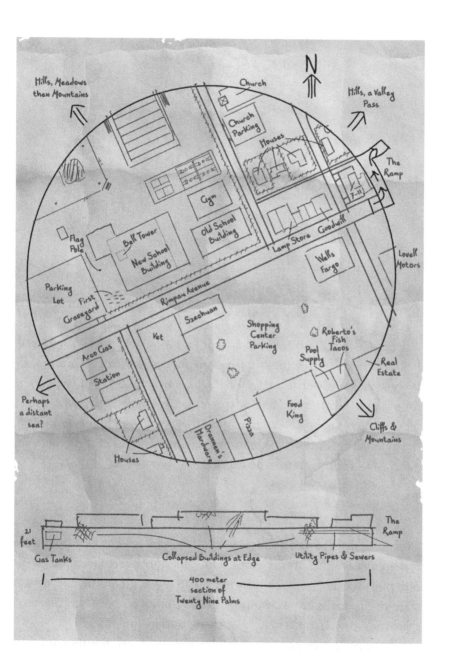

Hills, Meadows
then Mountains

Church

Hills, a Valley
Pass

N

Church
Parking

Houses

The
Ramp

7-11

Gym

Old School
Building

Lamp Store   Goodwill

Flag
Pole

Bell Tower

New School
Building

Wells
Fargo

Lovell
Motors

Parking
Lot   First
Graveyard

Rimpau Avenue

Szechuan

Shopping
Center
Parking

Roberto's
Fish
Tacos

Vet

Pool
Supply

Real
Estate

Perhaps
a distant
sea?

Arco Gas

Station

Food
King

Cliffs &
Mountains

Drommen's
Hardware

Pizza

Houses

21
feet

The
Ramp

Gas Tanks

Collapsed Buildings at Edge

Utility Pipes & Sewers

400 meter
section of
Twenty Nine Palms

13

EVALUATIONS

The first night was awful, although it started much better than Mark expected. The Ice Cream Fest and then the Great Big Burger Bash kept everyone occupied with a simulated holiday, as if something had happened worth celebrating. So there was some sense of well-being, even a little cheer, when the followers of Scott and Helene spread across the Rock, calling out a message to one and all. An invitation from Principal Jeffers to meet in the gym before dark — for planning and assessment of the situation.

And — for the many who wanted it — prayers.

THE POPULATION SPIKE that followed when Cirocco Labs set up the big research center at Twenty-Nine Palms had forced replacement of the old, ramshackle High School with one that was gleaming and new. A state-of-the-art campus helped draw employees out to Cirocco's research works in an arid land of cactus and Joshua trees.

Entering the gymnasium with his friends, Mark felt reassured by its massive cinderblock walls and double-pane glass. A long, hollow box, its plain walls bore only the electronic scoreboard and a few banners in TNPHS green and gold. Cool and fortresslike, it had been the first refuge of many dazed and confused students, who clustered together on the lower-left rows of fold-down bleacher seating, coaxed by Miss Williams, the guidance counselor. Some of them still wept or clutched one another, many hours into this interplanetary exile.

Another crowd clustered in very different spirit around Dave McCarty, who held court within a circle of admirers, squandering charge as he displayed image after image on his scroll-tab, showing off discoveries, like his map of the surrounding territory featuring freshly-named mountains. Plus images of native creatures: mostly those flyers with leathery or coarsely feathered wings and long, toothy beaks. Two girls elbowed each other competitively, till each of them won a native species, forever hers in fame.

Mark chuckled once, yet found the images disturbing. He wondered about those teeth. Heck, even plant-eaters might turn dangerous.

Take those insectoids – the Glow Wings... or Glowings – that seemed to gather in greater numbers by the hour. Mark watched one of them land on the back of his arm, while Alex and Barry scanned the bleachers for friends to sit with. The little creature was about the size of a large moth and – so far apparently — harmless. *They're drawn by something about humans, maybe our smell,* he pondered. Watching closely, he saw the creature unroll a tongue-like extension and tensed as it made contact with his skin. But there was no bite or penetration, just a gentle *licking,* as if delicately sampling the chemistry at the base of some hairs.

"Look," Barry nudged. "There's Conner and 'Cardo and the Hammar boys."

"Aren't you part of the science demonstration?" Alex inquired. Barry winced, then shrugged. And Mark realized, there were status wars among the nerds, as well. *Funny how the top thing we bring with us is our bad habits. Our hang-ups.*

Set in a square-cornered 'U', steep metal slat benches embraced the basketball court. The bleachers should have been full, with youngsters crammed in across the floor, as well, but not everyone had come. Mark felt sure at least a hundred kids - maybe two - were missing even after the crowd had been settled for about fifteen minutes, waiting for Principal Jeffers. The most shell-shocked students and townies might be unable to leave the classrooms where they were hiding.

There were also the guards outside, equipped now with two pistols and a deer rifle — all the firearms that anyone would admit to having. Mark suspected there must be more weapons in nearby homes or tucked under car seats in the parking lot, but Jeffers hadn't pushed it.

And maybe some had stayed outside to watch a new sun go down. The strangely mauve glow of this world's twilight penetrated broad, high windows lining what had been the north side of the gym. *So I guess that must be west now,* Mark thought. *Ah well.*

Frankly, they were all lucky even to have an indoor space like this, after the snatch across a galaxy and getting dropped onto an alien planet. Designed to California earthquake standards, the school buildings had all survived the shock pretty well, though several nearby houses seemed ready to collapse.

"Do you think they'll hit the lights?" Barry asked. "There are generators, I think. The carnival definitely has some."

"If it was up to me, I'd save fuel," Alex said.

Mark only shrugged, listening to the endless other questions all around him—

"—gonna start already?"

"Where do we sleep?"

"Sleep? What are we going to *eat* for Christsake?"

"Don't take His name in vain."

"Oh, shut up, Susie, I wasn't even—"

"You think it's true that some people are already leaving the rock? I heard some of the skateboard guys did it just to piss off Mr. Flatley."

The Rock. A good name for a stronghold. Or – didn't it used to stand for a famous prison? *We'll only be as strong as we make ourselves,* he thought. *Look at us. Look at me.* Everyone had kept close to their best friends, and with the student body stacked up here in the gym, old divisions were even more apparent, the bleachers spread with a patchwork of "tribes" — jock, geek, surfer, X, barbie, even goths, yup.

The core of the TNPHS climbing team sat with Mark, Alex, Barry, the Hammars, along with several X Kids and some of Barry's math club friends. Hayashi had a strange look on his face. *I'll have to ask Froggi if he really was crazy enough to hop over the side.*

Sure it was natural to cling to friends, in a time of crisis. But tribalism could also be a recipe for disaster. Mark knew he should have made more of an effort today to reach out, making sure people were okay instead of just running around to keep himself busy.

Sorry, Dad. I can do better. I will.

Abruptly – with an ominous pop and flicker — the gymnasium lights came on, a welcome flood that overpowered the windows' disturbing purple twilight. Powerful symbolism, this was what Denzel Jeffers must have planned.

The surrounding babble dropped to a low murmur as the principal entered at half-court along with Mr. Castro; Mrs. Swain, who taught English; three members of the student council, including Scott Tepper; and Bryant Marshall, a short, dark block of a man who owned the Chevy dealership. The rest of the staff stood or sat on a row of folding chairs along the far wall, or among the student body. The crowd of students and townspeople let out a low, happy murmur with some applause, although Alex muttered and shook her head, disapproving of wasted electricity. Especially when the Channel Six reporter and her tech stepped right in front of the teachers and student leaders – and suddenly the gymnasium scoreboard came alight with zoom-holo images of the principal.

The psychological boost is worth spending a little gas, Mark thought, no matter that he'd risked his life for what they were burning in the generators right now.

Jeffers strode in a short hook to face every part of the gym.

"Okay! Let's get started!" The acoustics were fine for his booming voice and Jeffers' footsteps clopped a steady, confident beat as he passed the front row of Mark's section, then paced methodically to his left, never stopping. "Can you all hear me!" Jeffers called, beckoning with both arms.

"YAAAAAAAAA!"

A thousand voices surged in answer and Mark felt goose bumps down his neck. His own voice seemed to push out of him with a will of its own. Grinning, Jeffers put a hand to one ear, indicating everyone should try again.

"Yeah! WHOOOOOO!" This time even Alex gave it everything she had. Encouraged by their own noise – and perhaps by an ice-cream high — it became a wild, echoing surge. Jeffers pumped his fist and yelled himself, turning to the faculty and student leaders, waving them to their feet. Scott Tepper gestured to Helene and to Colin Gornet and the football squad. They and the JV team roared back at him: "Spooks! Spooks! Twenty-nine spooks!"

At least as many cheerleaders, girlfriends, and coaches took up the TNPHS fight song, joined by kids all over the stands.

"—nine, *twenty-nine*—"

Stunned by his own reaction, Mark joined in, singing the words aloud for the first time in his life.

> *"Always rising to the fight!*
> *Do or die, day or night!*
> *Twenty-Nine Palms ..."*

It was hokey — so "Friday lunch" — pathetically dumb, a patriotic love-in at the end of the world. And it felt perfect, with Jeffers belting louder than anybody. Even Barry, who'd never attended a pep rally, stomped and clapped and blinked back tears. Alex cried outright and she was far from alone. The raised voices held a tinge of sobbing now, the decibel level falling but still fierce, full of terror and triumph together.

Hysterical release, Mark figured. He had seen it among Marines, back from patrol in Ecuador. Still, he marveled. *Could Jeffers really have it down so well? Using such simple tricks to bring us together? To yank us out of shock?*

How lucky. For the chain of respect and authority to be so clear at the start, leading to someone who was liked by everybody, or at least respected. No *Lord of the Flies* here. No collapse of being civilized. And so what if his appointed committees ignored the kids who took action at the very start. And so what if Jeffers's major domo was the smarmy-charismatic Scott. At least they were solid committees, appointed by a man who knew and cared for everybody.

Mark glanced up to the girder beams of the gymnasium, wondering.

Are there alien monitoring devices up there? Too small for us to detect, or invisible in some other way... are they watching and scanning, to see how we manage?

The possibility that this was all some kind of *Garubis experiment* – a test of "larval humans under stress" – had surely occurred to others among the castaways. *If so, are we doing better than you expected?*

Dozens of hands reached out and Principal Jeffers touched them or traded high-fives or "flu shakes," bonking fists, pausing to pat a shoulder or ruffle someone's hair. Once, a girl grabbed him and he had to peel her off, gently, with a laugh.

He's like a rock star down there.

Or maybe our Moses.

At last, Jeffers waved for quiet. Far more quickly than would have happened back home, he was obeyed. The gym was suddenly hushed. Mark looked at the tense young faces around him, rapt with anticipation and desperate hope.

"I'd like to thank you all for coming here on a week night ."

Jeffers grinned at the ensuing laughter and groans.

"I expect the teachers will agree that we can give everyone a pass on this evening's homework assignments."

Among the seats at half-court, Mr. Castro made a show of

smacking his palm against his head at the lousy joke. Edgy teens laughed again.

It's gonna work out, Mark thought. *Despite everything. This planet may kill us, but not because we fell apart.*

Only, that burst of confident optimism didn't last. For in the last row, to Mark's left, an adult with unfamiliar features, dressed in denim... one of the carnies, perhaps... was arguing viciously with Miss Najarro, his finger straight out between them like a knife.

It was only a few seconds, before the big man swiveled and stalked away, but with a snarl that said: *this ain't over.*

DOWN ON THE GYMNASIUM FLOOR, levity gave way to business.

"I know everyone has worries and questions!" Principal Jeffers called, even as he held up his hands again to forestall the rumble of voices. "So, before we go to committee reports, let me address some of the most pressing problems—"

"*I'm diabetic!*" shouted a Latino boy in the third row, sounding more angry than afraid. "Where's my insulin coming from?"

That set off others.

"I was having pins in my leg removed next week———"

"My mom works nights and needs me to babysit!"

"Sure, just —" Jeffers tried quelling with both hands, but that first spark ignited dozens.

"—my orthodontist—"

"—my therapist—"

"I had an audition—"

"I'm almost out of meds!"

So fast, Mark thought. He looked left and right to see if he could help calm anyone down. Miss Najarro had caught up with the carny, a wire-limbed man in Levis and a blue-and-white shirt, putting a restraining hand on his arm — which he brushed off with real force, making the teacher gasp.

"Bam, no," Alex said, grabbing his elbow.

Principal Jeffers was offering assurances. "Anyone with a medical condition, we do have a *big* supply of pharmaceuticals, a registered nurse and Doc Hutnicki from the clinic across the street, now that she's recovered from a fall."

That might be a bit of a stretch, Mark noted. It was a *veterinary* clinic, although sometimes Doc Hutnicki taught in the school's biology lab.

"—and Ms. Takka has a brand new *MolecuMac3000* in her biology classroom! So with any luck we should be able to synthesize –"

"We'll die here!" a girl screamed suddenly from somewhere to the left.

This time the interruption echoed into stunned silence ... till the same plaintive voice wailed on, each word feeling like a punch to the stomach.

"We're all gonna *die* in this place ... and I want to go home!"

Even Jeffers was left blinking ... till a sardonic voice from somewhere to Mark's right muttered – "Get that girl some more ice cream."

That drew smirks and cackles, breaking the tension. Then Dave McCarty countered. "Yeah, like five gallons of Peppermint Prozac."

More snarky chuckles, though Alex murmured a low growl next to him. "That's just plain mean."

Principal Jeffers spread his arms wide and got help from many in the audience, who made shushing sounds.

"I promise, finding answers and hopefully a way home will be top priorities, after survival ... and we *will* survive!" He punched the air with determination that won a weak round of applause. "Only, now let's hear from our committees. There's a lot to get done tonight and even more tomorrow. Everyone is needed to pitch in." He turned to the physics teacher. "Let's start with a report from Mr. Davis on what we know about our new home —"

Bad choice of words. Mark winced. Perhaps some castaways – had started taking up the attitude Dave McCarty avidly pioneered, absorbing the harsh possibility of permanent exile and calling it something else — *pioneering*. But for the rest, it was much too soon. The phrase only triggered moans of despair and outrage.

As Davis stepped forward with Ms. Takka and several students, including Dave with his precious map-scroll, a new voice rang out, this one older, angrier. "I'm not even supposed to be here! I was just driving past on Rimpau. I don't belong here with this stupid school!"

Pudgy and red-faced in a rumpled suit, the balding man's resentment was both illogical and ... it set off a similar thought in Mark. *What if Dad and I never came to Twenty-Nine Palms? What if ...*

The thin carny to his left stood upon the crowded bleachers, shouting in a commanding bark that carried across the gym. "I want to know who put you freaking *teachers* in charge!" he yelled. "You cleaned out the drugs and liquor and took most of the food! Who gave you the right?"

"Damn straight," growled another man from the aisle below — one of the local bikers, in a scarred leather jacket. "I'm not takin' orders from kids or their babysitters."

Mark saw the first carny try to push by Miss Najarro. It was like a rough dance move, the man's thin body eclipsing hers. Miss Najarro was only five-four and barely rounded top or bottom, as small as some of her freshman girls. Still, she caught at the man's shirt and he barked one word, harsh but indistinct in all the noise.

Mark stood up.

"Sit down," Alex said.

Most of the kids around Miss Najarro were first-year students, shrinking from the confrontation, uncertain and tense. Even the bravest sagged in relief as the carny turned away to join the man in leather, then both headed for the gym floor. Others stumbled through the packed bleachers as teenagers in their way protested.

"What were you going to do?" Alex hissed. "Punch him? How would that help?"

"She's right," Barry said quickly.

She is. Again. I guess.

Mark took his seat and yet his body felt tightly coiled with adrenaline, a ragged flood of dread and confidence, both dark and good, as loud as the gym around him. Somehow he tamped it down, avoiding his friends' eyes.

The noise-level dropped as a cluster of maybe a dozen angry adults hit the base of the stairs. Principal Jeffers was facing the other direction, both hands out as if to catch an immense section of the bleachers, but Mr. Castro left his chair. And suddenly Scott Tepper gestured at the football squad. They responded swiftly, with hefty Colin Gornet in front. No longer the richest kid in school, Gornet had size and plenty of other assets.

The carnies and other rough men hesitated. So did Principal Jeffers, who turned and stared as Scott's small army filled the middle of the floor. At the same time, Mr. Castro strode very close to the adults, talking urgently.

This could spiral out of control. Still, Mark couldn't help feeling impressed by Scott's poise. And envious for the loyal teammates he had at beck and call.

"What a derp mess," Barry said softly.

Mark could only nod and grimace. *It's happening to all of us, like crazy is wired in our brains. But maybe this is as good as it gets in a rough situation, two steps forward and one step back. We're as dangerous to ourselves as anything else might be.*

"Look," Alex said. "The bulge in that guy's back."

Mark followed her point and spotted the outline ... a protrusion under the spine of the carny's jacket. Probably a big knife. He hoped that was all.

Still talking rapidly, Mr. Castro gestured like a magician trying to distract attention. The history teacher and a dozen carnies and townspeople formed a triangle against the bulk of Scott's teammates. Principal Jeffers spoke to Scott, who then turned to motion his crew back to their seats, though Gornet and another big lineman stayed on the gym floor like bodyguards.

As if by agreement, the carnies backed off, too. They retreated as far as the nearest line of seats, where they stood with their arms crossed.

"All right!" Principal Jeffers yelled. "All right, first things first!" He was pacing again, trying to involve the entire crowd. "I appreciate there are others who got grabbed up along with the school. *Obviously* we'll have to work out ways to ... govern ourselves that seem fair to all. Yes? Meanwhile, though, stuff does have to get done and information has to be shared. We do have some ad hoc committees who have done good work. So how about we just get on with it and all pull together?"

Nods from the crowd. A couple of the protesting adults sat down. Mark sighed. The complaining students had a less-blustery tone, more whiney, but the message from old and young was the same. *I don't like this. Make it stop. Put things back the way they were.*

How do you make an interstellar adventure boring? Call up committees.

When the Security Group wanted more volunteers for patrols and look-outs, the shop guys stood up and protested. "You're already doing nothing useful! Strutting about with flimsy spears while we're building latrines and shoring up tottering houses."

"We have no idea what's out there!" Gornet shouted back.

"Yeah? And why must there be guards on the new latrines?"

"Hey, toilet paper rationing has gotta be enforced! Anyway, those rickety shit perches you built leave our butts exposed over alien jungle! Who knows what could jump and bite someone's ass, if we don't stand watch?"

Scott Tepper's smooth compromise, that the guards would take turns and do some other tasks too, calmed that tussle. But what about the shell-shocked, sheltering in dark rooms? Should they also be made to work? Some shouted for tough love, getting them outside. But a vote of hands supported Ms. O'Brien, who was carefully monitoring some of the most distraught students and adults. The stricken would get another day.

Mr. Jeffers used his veto power to quash another matter. The *alcohol proposal* died without a vote. Though everyone knew it would be back.

The Resource Committee's report was grim. An inventory of supplies could take days or even weeks, but preliminary estimates told what everyone already knew. Food and water would get scarce pretty darn soon. Moreover, several homeowners objected loudly to calls for sharing. One threatened to "shoot any putz kid with a clip-board who tries to get into my pantry!"

The standoff only broke when some Physics Club guys came trooping in from the dark, outside, bearing news that lifted Mark's interest.

"Twenty-eight hours and roughly twenty minutes," Mr. Davis announced the length of a full day, here on – *we'll need a name for this world,* Mark abruptly realized. "That's a lot longer than on Earth. Longer working days and longer nights. Also, this place seems to have a bigger axial tilt than Earth – we know because we spotted three other planets! That let us measure the angle from this solar system's ecliptic to our... well we have a North Star, folks."

"What does that mean?" Jeffers asked. One of the students rushed in an answer.

"It means hotter summers and colder winters!"

Mr. Davis nodded. "Seems likely."

"Do we know which season we're in?" A girl in the front row asked.

"No. That'll take several days to determine, I think."

Interesting, though not among the chief concerns. A different batch of science-types stepped up and soon had everyone leaning forward, hoping for good news. The senior biology teacher, Ms. O'Brien had once been a U.S. Navy medic, and thus far too busy, all day, dealing with crises among the human population. That left it to her junior, Miss Takka, and members of the various Bio Clubs – Future Health Workers of America, 4-H and the FIRST Genomics team — to offer up what they had learned about this world. Their report was disappointingly sparse.

"We captured some bug-like things," the young teacher began. "And used a pole to grab some leaves. We then offered them to ... offered them to ..."

Stammering, she couldn't continue. So a senior named Gracie

Donner — one of the soccer-gals, Mark recalled – gently pulled the teacher aside and took over.

"We've got a couple of gene and chemical sifters. But they were set up for standard high school classes," she said. "What with all their pre-sets and privacy filters, the results have been skimpy. Mostly, the damn machines keep trying to give us failing grades on a lab." That got a couple of wry laughs.

"We're hoping the local veterinarian, Doc Hutnicki, can help us out, since her machines aren't ... child-proofed. But she's recovering from a concussion she suffered when we first arrived. For now, it could take a while to reconfig our machines ... to change their settings to analyze how life works here. If any of you are hackers or electronics types, we could use help."

Barry Tang didn't hesitate. He stood and headed forward, along with half a dozen others. *Good,* Mark thought. *Barry needs a way to feel useful.*

Gracie continued. "Thanks, guys. Meanwhile? We've set up some terrariums and started feeding some leaves and local fruits to some of the hamsters from the pet store. Some of the stuff they won't touch, so I guess we shouldn't either. Other samples, they dig right in! Still, it's way too soon to tell if that means anything good. Even if they're all alive tomorrow –" She shrugged.

"We need more samples. So, in the morning, some volunteers need to go down there —" from her head nod, everyone knew she meant the world below.

Dave McCarty almost leaped out of his seat, but Gracie cut him off. "I will choose a team, after this meeting ends."

Mark and Alex shared a look. *Wow. Decisive.*

Equally firm were the two Vice Principals. Mrs. Swain, who also taught English, declared that the gym would become a girls' dorm. After this meeting ended, volunteers would pass out blankets. She then added, in a firm voice, that she and some other adult chaperones planned to be old-fashioned and prudish about sex — "to a degree you've never seen before, except maybe in old time movies, or in books like *The Scarlet Letter.* I mean it girls! The stupidest thing you can do right now is get pregnant, before we know more about our lives here. If this presents a problem, come see me and I'll listen like a big sister. But don't try me."

Mr. Lavallee was even blunter. The gruff, ex-sergeant served as both Vice Principal and varsity coach. He leaned on a cane to favor his prosthetic leg. "Any young man who lets instinct overcome his brain, and pushes himself onto others, without attention to consent or consequences, *will* face something *far* more than old-fashioned, from me." And the cane came up. To Mark's surprise, the threat was greeted with only a few muttered sneers, and those cut off swiftly, as most of the assembled students nodded.

There were other committees – a seemingly endless list of them – but Principal Jeffers could clearly see his audience was fading. Everyone suffered from a combination of physical fatigue, emotional exhaustion and delayed ice-cream letdown. Still, the tussles weren't over. As part of some compromise worked out with Mr. Castro, the leader of the carnies, the thin man, Zach Serpa, was given the floor. He seemed calmer now, but still pulled compulsively at his hands, explaining that his people would share and cooperate ... even contribute members for some of the committees, though without accepting that Jeffers had any overall authority.

He also proclaimed a territorial boundary, making the south end of the athletic field off limits to students, or to anyone else lacking permission. "We don't want any more kids sneaking through our set-up stealing stuff!"

So they had a real grievance after all, Mark realized.

"That's no good," protested Bryant Marshall, owner of the Chevrolet dealership ... what was left of it. He had been sitting close to Jeffers, lending support. "They're better supplied than anyone else on this rock. They've got propane- or battery-powered refrigerators in those carnival trailers — *full* refrigerators! And mini stoves, showers and beds and extra clothes. Generators and fuel. Motors and pumps. Canvas, rope, and lumber. Barrels of junk food and drinks."

Marshall was ignoring urgent looks from the history teacher, whose deal with the carnies seemed to unravel with every word.

"Tell me, Mr. Serpa. Is it your plan to keep all of that to yourselves?"

Fuming and short of breath, Serpa shouted. "It's *your* good luck ... and our *bad luck* ... that we happened to be here for your damned *Desert Carnival!*"

"This is no time to let one group set itself apart –"

"Yeah? Watch us! I caught a couple of jerk-jocks standing by our corral, talking about how much meat there was on our donkeys and the llamas! I showed 'em what to expect, if they come back!"

So many were watching the spittle, flying from the grizzled carnie's mouth, that perhaps no one else noticed his hand reaching around toward the bulge, under the denim jacket. Mark stood, preparing to leap —

— when Alex shot up and did something that took Mark completely by surprise.

"No donkeys!" She screamed, at the top of her lungs, drawing all eyes her way. "We won't eat your donkeys! Poor donkeys. Poor donkeys. Poor donkeys ..."

Amid some frantic giggles, others took up the chant.

"Poor donkeys! Poor donkeys!"

Mark had seen it before. Near murderous tension, broken by a moment of hysterical relief. Only this time it wasn't achieved by a diplomat or soldier or teacher, but a coltish 15-year old.

"Poor donkeys! Poor donkeys!"

Alex cast him a sidelong grin, as the chant took off without any further help. A mantra of utter nonsense, soon lost to even its original meaning, as laughter mixed with sobs. And everyone knew who the 'donkeys' were, deserving pity for a fate that was not at all their fault.

We are the donkeys. Poor us.

Mark didn't let his wound-up muscles relax till he saw the man in denim bring his hand back around – empty. Serpa nodded acceptance to the shouting students, attempting a stern smile, though his eyes said *this isn't over.*

No, it isn't, Mark thought. He was thinking ahead. Even if the carnies shared their supplies fairly, and even if the Garubis "gift" of this world meant there was food to be had, he knew harsh days were ahead. And donkey meat might yet be on the menu. And llama. And hamster.

And then, maybe, us.

Principal Jeffers made no effort to regain an agenda, clearly recognizing the time had come to close. Taking control again with raised arms, he simply ended on a hopeful note.

"Good night, and God bless us all."

EVEN UNDER IDEAL CONDITIONS, the squeeze to empty the bleachers was never pretty. Migration out of the gym was even clumsier as a majority wanted out on one side, through doors leading to the main building, where a table staffed by volunteers offered each person one rationed cup of water. A guide path of solar lanterns illuminated long lines at the makeshift latrines, though a lot of the boys headed off in the dark to one of the open storm drains, along Rimpau.

Alex held back, briefly surrounded by a few admirers who patted her on the back, or shook her hand, for defusing the tense situation. Mark watched, proud of her, but above all surprised by how unsurprised he was. *Well, I always figured she was special.*

Yet his gaze drifted to Gracie Donner, gathering her team of biologists and guards for tomorrow's expedition. *That's where I belong.* And yet, he held back, watching as Helene Shockley managed the long line allocating blankets. The youngest kids were handed those first. But when it came the turn of juniors and seniors, by almost silent agreement among the boys – maybe some kind of chivalry reflex learned from old movies – the guys plucked up tarps and painters' dropcloths from the hardware store, leaving all remaining blankets for the older girls. And no one raised it as an issue.

Under the watchful eye of Mrs. Swain, some hetero couples clung tearfully before separating in opposite directions in search of someplace not too hard or cold. To collapse.

A few went the other way, including Froggi, Greg and Nick. "Meet us at our spot in twenty minutes!" Froggi said, and Mark nodded, wondering what they had in mind.

Our spot. That must be the climbing wall.

With that, the Hammar boys pushed open the wide doors at what had been the gym's north end, letting in a current of strange air, refreshingly cool after the heat of so many bodies, yet tinged with the acid vinegary jungle aroma. At least it pushed aside the stink of a thousand filthy teenagers, with showers right in this building but zero water to spare.

Alex sent her last freshman admirer scooting toward Women's Country, but seemed in no hurry to join that purdah. Mark told her of the rendezvous. *Unless I'm mistaken, they want to organize our own dawn patrol into the forest.*

"Wait!" Barry called, and Mark slowed down enough for them to regroup. Barry seemed much happier now, chattering about his long night ahead. The hackers would be issued unlimited caffeine, in hope of reconfiguring the bio-assay machines by tomorrow morning. The prospect invigorated him, until a sight abruptly rendered Barry speechless.

Stars. Unknown stars. Outside, a few meters beyond the gym lights, they seemed to swarm overhead like a sparkling wave. The clear sky, colored like gunmetal, seemed to spray hot pinpoints over-head, completely alien. Four of them seemed very close. One was a big, red ember.

"That's a planet," Barry said, almost whispering. "Dang, I can make out a disk, bare-eyed."

Mark gaped like a child. He stumbled as the pressure of more students made them step to the side.

I wonder if we're even in the Milky Way anymore.

"Look. A moon!" Barry pointed toward the west, where a narrow crescent hung above the horizon, at least twice the apparent width of Luna. "They said it was close, but man, it's big."

"So many stars," someone else gasped nearby, and these were desert kids, accustomed to decent skies. Mark noticed crowds gath-ering where the astronomy club had set up many instruments, at the far end of the plaza, chattering with more enjoyment than anybody ought to, if they'd just been kidnapped across a galaxy.

Yep. We are a really varied species of ape.

"There's another planet over there," Alex said, pointing in a different direction. Mark turned. Then screaming began somewhere in the twilight behind them.

14

VISITORS

It was a boy. Terror raised his voice into a screech, but Mark never doubted the screamer was male. His instant, worried guess: one of the big jocks standing guard out at the edge.

"*Gaaaaaaaah!*"

He sounded hurt. Also brave, because the cry twisted into words before cutting off.

"*Bats! Bats! RUN! Bats! They're —*"

The clarity that Mark had felt, absorbing the new sky, stayed with him as he turned — not to escape, but to help. That would have been a mistake. Two things saved him.

There were people everywhere in the shadowy space between the gym and the main wing of the school, milling around bike racks and raised planters as they tried to fit into one line or another. One column stretched from the nurse's office inside the main wing out to the flag pole. Another, leading back into the locker rooms was another zigzag mess.

These formations shattered as the guard screamed, as a maelstrom of bodies barred Mark's path. Worse, the gym doors rattled open again as several dozen girls came out to investigate. Some instinct told him to look up.

The night rippled, as if the surrounding forest horizon lifted and then fell on a sudden wind. A *cloud* rushed over them, and darkness became a solid, biting thing, filled with screams.

Bats? Mark had a brief impression of spasming black worm-like things — small, no bigger than his thumb, with wings about the size of his hand and long, thin, cutting tongues that stabbed and darted in the moonlight. Their only noise was a staccato rustling of frenzied motion, soon lost in a rising roar of human cries. The wave of dark fliers rushed past him like ten thousand needles stitching through paper as the savage little creatures formed swells and bunches, almost like deliberate knives, dividing the crowd. And he realized —

They're isolating some of the smaller kids.

Even as he moved, Mark recognized the pattern, like a school of piranha, or a pack of wolves, culling out and then taking down cornered animals. The crowd surged again as everyone ran, hundreds of voices echoing from the tall cinderblock walls.

Mark bumped uselessly against the panicked mob, one step, two, trying to reach a freshman girl lost in a jittering cyclone of wings, but he was struck in the hip and then in his ribs. Arms and elbows, everywhere. He staggered as the human stampede turned him toward the gym.

The change of direction, giving in to the group impulse, went through Mark with much deeper force than the impacts against his body. Heart pounding, his body and mind trembled with adrenaline. His first thought was loud and wild, full of anger at himself. *If you'd run out there you might have died.*

Then he looked for Alex.

Where is she?

Searching for his friends in the gloom, Mark slammed into several mountain bikes chained to a rack, scraping his ankle and stomach.

Something whispered against his hair. He ducked and threw an awkward swat, maybe hurting one or two of the swarming creatures. A stiff little body smacked into his knuckles, feeling a lot like a hackeysack, and further down his arm a dry mass of wings crumpled against the bones of his wrist.

That was when pain began.

Mark choked and twisted away from his own left arm. He banged his shoulders and lower back against the hard protrusions of two bikes and was hardly aware of it. His world had closed down to one bright jagged spike of horror and he threw his arm from side to side into tires and metal struts and gears, frantic to get the bat off.

The palsied monster was humping and squirming. Somewhere under a tent of wings were tiny claws, four or six or more, scratching at him like fine needles, but it was the whipcord tongue that made him yell. It unfurled like an oily pink wire and cinched completely around his wrist, breaking the skin, squeezing his tendons and muscle.

The bat-thing's eyes were yellow beads.

It was hot and stank of musk and droppings.

Mere seconds passed before the agony in Mark's arm changed, perhaps from a natural anesthetic in the creature's saliva. It left him more aware of the severe bruises he was inflicting on himself but he didn't stop, bashing his arm down on the bike's ridged gears again and again.

Mark had no way of knowing if the toxin would paralyze or kill him if it reached his heart or brain. Yet fear was overwhelmed by greater emotions. Duty to his friends. And revenge. The bat clung to him even in death and he ripped at its broken wings, feeling one claw let go. His fingers were slick with its thin, dark blood and his left hand wasn't working well, but he finally peeled the ugly thing away as he turned.

At least a hundred students and adults jammed entrances to the gym and main building, shrieking, flailing blindly at the haze of bats. Four sets of doors just weren't enough. He saw an adult trip over one boy's feet. Both of them went down and the boy dragged someone else with him.

Yet, the tumult at the doors had benefits. The bat-things whirled and slashed over the mob, yet curled away from the howling turbulence of heads and arms. In well-defined, arrow-like swirls, they retreated from the heart of the crowd. The tiny monsters were feeling out the shape of the stampede, cutting people away from the back end in ones and twos, like a hideous, lashing tide. Teens screamed and flailed with jackets and backpacks, and some of the predators fell.

They always from come above, he noted, squirming out of his own jacket and waving it like a helicopter blade, over his head. *Never from the side.*

We need shields. Armor. Clubs. Lacrosse sticks, football helmets, shoulder pads, even blankets might work. *If I could only get to the equipment room. Heck, umbrellas would be great!* As if there were many of those, in good old Twenty-Nine Palms, Mojave Desert, California.

The darkness added to the chaos. Peeling away from the door jam, in their terror students careened into each other, channeled by the raised planters and bike racks— A blond girl, with a lick of blood across her temple—

An adult man, hunched over to make himself smaller than the children—

We have to get out of here, Mark thought. *Head for other doors.*

Unable to keep whirling the jacket, he wrestled it overhead, kept his elbows bent and let the fabric stretch against his scalp and shoulders, like a sail. Doing this exposed his torso, but it also gave him extra protection where it counted most. Bat-things swooped, but only hit his left hand and the empty decoy of the jacket.

"This way!" he shouted into the white face of a junior he recognized — Cammie Rosa — she had wisps of blood-wet hair stuck to her ear and cheek. "Tell everyone! This way! We'll go around the main wing!"

Incomprehension flashed through Cammie's eyes, swiftly replaced by a glint of steel — and he saw she was attached to another girl, one hand clenching her friend's wrist. They made a daisy-chain of three, with the last girl sobbing back over her shoulder for someone else they'd lost in the screaming dark.

Mark turned to holler at two more kids. "Your jackets! Over your head! Like this!"

Cammie started yelling, too, luring more students to form into her chain. Groups glommed together. In less than a minute, twenty-five or more were shuffling past the flagpole, most of them with a shirt, a jacket, a purse, a backpack over their heads. The knot of teenagers became large enough that a spearhead swarm veered away, seeking stragglers.

Mark shouted at two seniors who'd burrowed to the center of the group. "Smaller kids in the middle! You two keep everyone moving. Around the cafeteria. I'm going after others."

Even as he yelled, Mark looked back at the gym, thinking the doors must have cleared.

But what he saw made his heart plummet.

One set of doors was closed! The double-doors on the far right had been shut, despite the horde of people clamoring to get in. Students and adults trampled each other to move left, toward the remaining set. For an instant, Mark thought he saw Alex, her wiry frame struggling to hold a door open against much larger bodies. The sight froze him. But he knew hesitation was death.

"That way!" he yelled at Cammie and a skinny kid with glasses who seemed to have it together. While they cajoled the growing convoy forward, Mark dashed over to three hunched forms huddled by a planter. Mark used his jacket to disperse a swarm, then to whack feeding bat-things off their victims. It took strength to yank the kids out of their fetal balls and then send them stumbling toward Cammie. The skinny guy had guts, running forth to retrieve the trio, screaming like a banshee as he whirled his own jacket, using it also to drive the wounded ones along.

Another pair of stragglers hurried over when Mark called. But a third group wasn't so lucky. Mark had to carry a wounded boy while others clutched his belt. That left Mark's jacket hanging from his head like a hoodie, with bat-oid things crawling across, seeking an opening. They departed only when Mark's rescues reached the comparative safety of the herd.

"Stay together!" Cammie shouted. "It's not far! We're going for the offices around to the left!" Kids banged against each other, cursing, stumbling, yet they reached the immense flat shape of the main building and got some respite. The batties were incredibly nimble, but the building should offer some cover.

Fifty meters, he thought. *It can't be more than a fifty, can it?*

It was a perfect nightmare. A dart of bats across his face. A wailing kid who ran past the convoy without seeing or realizing its partial safety. Mark tried to find the energy to chase after the poor fellow, and found that he had no reserves. Across the quad, he saw a body unmoving on the concrete.

Someone – he never knew who – took the wounded kid from his arms. Maybe he could walk now.

They were forced to waddle, knees bent but chests up to make their raised arms their highest points. Too many of them had naked backs or nothing more to protect them than a bra strap. One boy screamed when a bat lashed at his spine, and others cried out in fear. But having recovered from their panic, now two of the larger guys took turns patrolling the group, swatting predators, crushing them with bare hands. Of course that would only work until —

The thin guy pointed and shouted. "A big swarm... I think it's the main one. They look like... they've spotted us!"

We'll never make it to the doors. If only there was a window. Mark looked around desperately. He spotted more stragglers, six teenagers and an adult kneeling beside a Coke machine and another bike rack—

And a fire extinguisher.

Summoning some strength, Mark ran for it, breaking ranks. "Stay close to the wall! Keep moving!"

Wings skittered overhead. He ducked and yanked his shirt off entirely, making a rough wad of it in his left hand. His bad hand. He punched into the glass. On the third try, it shattered.

Somewhere an alarm went off, clanging above the din of voices. Battery-powered. *Awesome.* Mark hoped everyone on this hellish little island would realize what he'd done and make the connection themselves.

Barry and Alex and Froggi, he thought. *They'll know.*

If they're alive.

Two of the stragglers argued with each other, a girl pulling at a boy. "Please, let's join them! Please!" she cried, on her feet, but the boy stayed against the Coke machine with his rigid fingers clamped onto its red plastic, yelling, "We're safer here!"

The girl was exposed. The bats recognized it. An open black claw of spasming wings and tongues shot out of the night. It covered her head first, spiraling around her long hair and bangle earrings, tugging her off-balance away from the boy. Her delicate hands came up helplessly even as the bats began to twist her off her feet.

Mark swung the canister around and blasted the swarm with a loud shock of fire retardant. The girl fell hard on the concrete, bleeding but alive. She screamed as bats landed all around her and convulsed and twitched. Most of them leapt back into the sky. Mark crushed one with his shoe and felt another strike at his pantleg. The girl shoved herself onto her knees even before her boyfriend reached her.

"Oh, Shawn, oh my God—"

"Move it! Run!" Mark hollered as he hurried along the convoy of refugees, shooting brief bursts wherever the attackers seemed to be clustering on prey, breaking up concentrations, desperately hoping the ammo would hold. Night vision had kicked in. But other senses seemed more reliable — every hair on his body stood up as stiff as a pin, as if each one was a quivering nerve reaching away from him. The premonition of another attack was as real and sickening as his icy hot pulse.

It didn't come. He did dash over to blast a clump that almost covered two desperately flailing teens. A large student and one of the town citizens gathered the victims in their arms as Mark scanned about, ignoring bats that swept by in twos or threes.

"Let's go! Let's go!" The skinny kid with the glasses cried, urging everyone forward tight against the wall.

The bats only flittered into them once, trying to get to the girl. Her blood.

His mind raced.

The one that bit me, it was so hot. And that might be what drove them off — not just the blast itself or the noise, but because I coated them in powder.

They eat meat and blood. All protein. The powder might blind them. Hide us. It definitely hurts 'em.

"Oh—!" The boyfriend hesitated when he saw the door to the admin office, nearly tripping the girl and Mark.

The door was closed, and even in the night Mark could see a bulk of human shapes standing against it on the inside, pulling it shut. The top part of the door was glass. But the glass had been broken in one corner where they'd reached in to get the lock, and the skinny kid shouted, "Open up, open up!"

Mark let himself drop out of the group, staying low. He turned and squeezed off the last of the fire extinguisher, one blast at random, the second at a swirl in the dark. Then the extinguisher hissed and died.

People were yelling. He threw himself toward the sound.

They must have gotten the door open because hands clutched at his hair and his bad arm, yanking him inside where he fell. Then the door slammed. Glass danced on the tile floor close to his face and a girl shrieked, "You idiots! Cover the window with something!"

Mark scrambled out of the way as a dozen pairs of feet shuffled around him from different directions. Binders, keyboards, a big desk calendar were passed forward to plug the hole. Two guys upended an entire table in a deafening crash of computers and printers and shouted, "Watch out! Move!"

There was no time to rest. While some hunted down any bat-things that had come in, other voices echoed in the hallway behind the office, other survivors, sobbing and shouting. Mark pulled himself to his feet and against a wall. He tried to peer through the black-on-black shadows.

He needed help. He found the skinny kid easily. Each lens of the kid's square glasses held a smudge of moonlight that winked and went out when his face turned toward Mark.

"Holy shit, dude," the kid said, making a shaky noise that might have been a laugh.

"We need as many fire extinguishers as we can get," Mark told him. "There's still people out there."

～

THE BATOIDS (as some called them) were gone twenty minutes later. Someone marshaled a small gang of boys, girls, and two adults back into the darkness. They went through the main entrance in a tightly packed circle, armed with fire extinguishers, mops, brooms, and wearing wastebaskets for helmets or jackets wrapped like turbans around their heads. They were a big shuffling beast that gained more size as bleeding kids crawled out of hiding — from under benches, inside dumpsters or under huddles of clothes.

In the moonlight, the pavement seemed to squirm with wounded bats, like crumpled hunks of leather. In one spot they found fifty of the ugly things on the concrete, wheezing, barely moving. Mark didn't know what to make of it, but he didn't want to find out. He led the group in a wide detour around the patch of sluggish creatures.

A few human sounds dotted the darkness and small groups detached to reclaim wounded kids, guarded by sentries with fire extinguishers.

Leonard Kelly, the skinny kid, croaked, "Somebody oughta knock on the gym and tell them the party's over."

"Go for it, Leo," Mark whispered. The poor guy had probably been picked on for years for looking like a geek. Here was a well-earned chance for him to get limelight. "Tell 'em to grab all the extinguishers they have and come help."

They moved on, pulled a dazed boy to his feet and supported him between them as they continued.

The next fellow was less lucky, his throat open. Hundreds of little prints marked the edges of the bloody puddle. Wings. Claws. The swarms had intensified here. *Drawing attention away from others,* Mark thought, wondering if that made him cold-blooded.

Above them, the sky was so beautiful, clear and cool, with a million new stars and the giant moon.

"Anybody know who this is?"

Voices rose behind him as the gym doors clanked open. He felt glad – angry, exhausted, and glad. Two powerful flashlight beams stabbed out from a cluster of human shapes.

"Okay, let's keep moving this way," he said. He wanted to rest. He wanted to find Alex and Barry and Mr. Castro and Froggi and the twins ... and Helene ... and Dave and Charlie ... but if anyone else was still out here, they might be in desperate need of timely first aid.

The bats might come back, he thought. *We have to be ready. There's no telling what their normal patterns are, and we might have confused them as badly as they did us.*

The notion stayed with him as he crept forward, wishing he had one of those flashlights.

Then he stepped on another bat-thing and jumped. "Aah!"

This one was alive. A sophomore girl stepped out of the group to stomp it with her designer-heeled sandals.

He waved his group forward, hoping he might recognize his friends among the thin crowds filing out of the gym. Flashlights. Voices calling.

Great. Now you bring out the sports equipment, Mark mused, as a couple of dozen burly guys emerged all suited up in football pads, helmets, and gloves with towels packed in the joints. In an eclectic touch, they wielded baseball bats and proceeded to go after bat things that were flopping on the ground, while Grace Donner and a few of her bio gals dashed ahead of the vengeance squad, grabbing still-living ones to stuff into plastic jars. Two townies and a carnival man brandished shotguns.

Together, they took back the school grounds.

∾

ALEX FOUND him sharing the remnants of one small bottle of water with Leo and two other kids on a far corner of the gymnasium grandstand. She had a bruise rising on her left cheek, where a right-handed punch would have landed. Some panicking fool who tried slamming the gym door against refugees, Mark figured. Whoever it was, probably came out worse for the struggle. *I pity the fool.*

Alex also had a raw stripe on her neck where a bat licked her. He recalled the boy they'd seen whipped across the throat ... Another inch and Alex might have shared that fate.

She hugged him while he was still trying to make sense of his feelings. Good. She couldn't see his face with their arms around each other, and she started crying and Mark realized he couldn't breathe. Fortunately, Barry was there too and he punched Mark's shoulder in a very unBarry-like way.

They settled down together after Leo volunteered to get more water in the teeming chaos.

"Do you think they'll be back?" Alex asked.

"We're probably safe for the night, but I'm just guessing. The swarm probably pounced because ... well, they probably seldom see so many warm bodies, after dark."

"Yeah," Barry agreed. "There's no way any other native life would stay exposed at nightfall like we did. The natives must go to ground and wait out the bats, but there were so many of us ... I'll bet the bats usually gorge on their prey and then go home to digest and sleep."

"Then why ... the ones lying on the ground. So many of them looked just *lethargic*. Not injured, but they seemed more tired than the humans."

"Could be they were driven wild by how defenseless we seemed," Mark commented. "That kept them attacking and gorging, when normally they would've burned out after just a few minutes."

"And so they died." Barry nodded. "Ironic."

"We don't know what fraction died. A lot. But ... They must live near here. That's a problem." He shrugged. "Anyway, this disaster won't happen again. Now we know better."

Alex nodded. "One lesson learned. But at what cost?"

Mark could see Principal Jeffers, his face stricken as Ms. Takka, the younger biology teacher held out a clipboard, no doubt tallying the dead. Mark had only seen three, and heard of two more, including the guard who shouted the first warning. But he suspected darkly there'd be more.

Flexing his still half-numb left arm, Mark refrained from speaking aloud his other worry. He didn't have to. Everyone must be thinking the same thing.

What if the bites and tongue-licks are poisonous to humans?

The gym was overpacked again, with half the basketball court set aside as a makeshift hospital and frightened kids and adults stacked up through the bleachers. At least the lights were on again, no matter if they were burning up irreplaceable gas. Darkness would have been terrifying.

Mark spotted Mr. Castro helping with the wounded, but nobody had seen Dave McCarthy's black jacket or Charlie Escobar's big chin, or a lot of other people. Froggi and the twins were gone, too, but Mark didn't worry much about them. The X Kids had probably taken cover away from the rest of the population.

Out on the basketball court, some were being treated for neck wounds. Several wore bandages over an eye. One girl – both eyes. There were broken bones from falls ... and no lack of volunteer nurses.

I should help, he thought. And Mark knew that he was too spent to do anyone else the slightest good.

Nothing remained of the confident, almost cocky TNPHS spooky spirit, when the Grand Meeting had broken up. No one would soon forget how students, townies and carnies battled each other at the doors, some fighting to close them and others – like Alex – to keep open a way for refugees.

There were fractures throughout their community — mistrust and doubt — to say nothing of the bruises and bloody lips inflicted by each other.

Some "colony." We failed our first crisis, Mark thought.
We have to be able to rely on each other. It's all we've got.
No one slept well through the long, alien night.

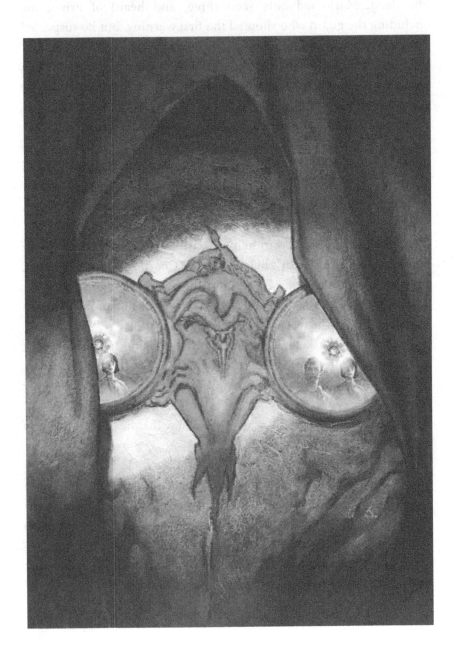

ADULT SUPERVISION?

Many of us wanted the assignment – to watch how Earthlings will do the inevitable. How they will waste the Great Gift that we have given them.

It happens every time that we do a favor for a young race, following rules laid down long ago by the absent Law-Givers. We are bound by ancient oaths, to fulfill obligations. Bound ... but if we fulfill the letter of the law, in our own way? The Law-Givers are gone, and we now satisfy our debts in whatever way might amuse the Garubis Polity.

On Earth, I bared this body of mine for capture and abuse by foolish human grubs. And their larvae behaved mostly as-predicted, with savage insensitivity to possible consequences. But some of them ... a few ... acted with surprising grace, saving this one's life. Saving my life. And so they spared their species from our fore-planned trap. Our retribution would have been justified and fierce –

— but instead, I lived. I was returned to the Garubis Bosom. And Retribution had to be set aside for a time, in favor of Reward. And from the list of prizes, we chose to give them a colony.

A settlement-refuge, for several hundred brooding-age human females and their attendant drones. For them to make the best of. Or to fail, according to their talents and moral character.

Having spent months among them, I know how the human adults and sages would complain over this gift. Had they been given just one day of warning, they might have gathered two thousand volunteers with a myriad skills and equipped with every clever tool to make this colony a success. And perhaps that is the way a Law-Giver would do things.

But the Law-Givers are gone. Leaving us behind, shackled by their laws.

Oh, but we Garubis have become fine lawyers!

Let the humans scream, mourning their lost spawn. Their rage will only make them more prone to error, when next we meet.

Meanwhile, we will watch this experimental brood nest of their soft, ill-disciplined hatchlings. Our simulations predict some amusing failure modes, as we observed happen to other gift-recipients, in the past.

Humiliated by my failure to be killed on Earth – shamed by receiving their kindness – I did not think I would win the prize I next sought — this assignment to watch the children fail, close-at-hand. But blood counts and my high caste prevailed, one more time. And so, I will supervise from shadows, relishing the painful ironies.

For revenge is the highest art. And we take payback seriously. And so we retaliate, time and again, against our Masters. By living according to the letter of their laws – but never the spirit.

So come now, human teens. Do not disappoint me.

As you would say: blow it.

End of Book One

ACKNOWLEDGMENTS

Grateful acknowledgement and thanks go to the fine folks at the Golden Duck Foundation and Reading for the Future, for inspiring me you write something for Young Folks, and to Robert Silverberg, Andre Norton, Robert Heinlein and others for inspiring me, much earlier.

And Bill Schafer of Subterranean Press for publishing the earlier, much shorter version of this story called Sky Horizon, a version that won the Hal Clement Award for best science fiction novel for Young Adults, in 2008. That version got substantial nibbles from Hollywood. Maybe this time...

And Scott Hampton for his terrific interior art and vivid cover for that SubPress edition.

And this round of sharp-eyed pre-readers, Steve Ruskin, Jennifer Claver, Roy Harvey, David Ivory, Jonathan Armstrong, Doug McElwain, Darrell Ernst and Duncan Cairncross, Steve Jackson, Matt Crawford and Bonnie Hartmeyer. And earlier Mark Grygier and Ari, Terren and Ben Brin.

And of course Cheryl Brigham, who also has wonderful stories to tell about youth and perseverance.

You too... go forth. Thrive and persevere..

ABOUT THE AUTHOR

David Brin is a scientist, tech speaker/consultant, and author. His novels about our survival and opportunities in the near future are *EARTH* and *Existence*. A film by Kevin Costner was based on *The Postman*. His 16 novels, including NY Times Bestsellers and Hugo Award winners, have been translated into more than twenty languages. *Earth*, foreshadowed global warming, cyberwarfare and the world wide web. David appears frequently on shows such as Nova and The Universe and Life After People, speaking about science and future trends. His non-fiction book -- *The Transparent Society: Will Technology Make Us Choose Between Freedom and Privacy?* -- won the Freedom of Speech Award of the American Library Association.

(Website: http://www.davidbrin.com/)

Made in the USA
Coppell, TX
03 October 2023